Following the directions of a mysterious, all-knowing dowager, H G (Hope Grace) Wells and Doctor Peter Rhodes (from The Institute) break out two male prisoners from jail and together with an investigative reporter, her female companion, and a tough, no-nonsense female detective (all five from The Program) take them back in time from 2018 Melbourne to their 1898 London.

H G is the younger cousin of the famed author H. G. Wells—the other H G as she calls him—and the foremost physicist of the late Victorian era. Their mission, with the aid of their contemporary companions from Melbourne, to rescue Peter's kidnapped wife Samantha.

This leads to an incredible, dangerous, and at times brutal story of abductions, rescue, time travel, savagery, love, romance, and dematerialisations involving characters such as Jack the Ripper and Robert the Bruce, as H G and her companions travel along their predestined paths. This strange and at times mystical tale is weaved together by a new and improved space/time machine called the DEMAT, designed by H G and her great friend, the abducted woman Mrs. Samantha Rhodes, who, like H G, is a brilliant physicist.

All five time travellers from the twenty-first century are fated to fulfil their own, individual destinies, while at the same time unwittingly ensuring certain historical events take place along the way. Their journeys, along with that of H G's, dictated to by the written instructions of the mysterious dowager.

Predestined
Copyright © 2019 Stephen Mottram
ISBN: 978-1-4874-2376-6
Cover art by Martine Jardin

Published by eXtasy Books Inc or
Devine Destinies, an imprint of eXtasy Books Inc

Look for us online at:
www.eXtasybooks.com or www.devinedestinies.com

PREDESTINED
A SEQUEL TO THE PROGRAM
AND THE INSTITUTE

BY

STEPHEN MOTTRAM

Prologue

London 1897

Hope Grace Wells—or H G as she was known to her friends—was shocked as she read the short, typed message delivered to her that morning. *If you want your machine to become a reality, then come to the above address at two this afternoon.*

My machine? How could they possibly know about that? Her time machine was still a concept, a project she and her best friend and fellow physicist, Samantha Rhodes, were working on.

Her older cousin, Herbert George Wells—the other H G as she liked to call him—had written a bestseller called *The Time Machine* some two years prior. But that was pure fantasy, a rollicking adventure for readers to enjoy, nothing at all to do with her enterprise.

She was confused by the missive, but one thing was clear. She must accept the messenger's request, her determined, intelligent mind certain that time travel was far more than a possibility—that it was inevitable.

CHAPTER ONE

London 1898

Hope Grace Wells — H G to her friends — sat beside Samantha Rhodes, her best friend and colleague, as they strapped themselves into the machine. They wore their bonnets and gloves, determined to present themselves immaculately for when, and if, they arrived at their destination.

Samantha looked across the pod nervously. "This is it, H G, the culmination of our dreams."

With her usual determination, H G displayed no such nerves. "It will work. Of this, I have no doubt." She had good reason to feel confident. Her mentor and guide, a veiled, secretive dowager had said it would, and until then, the woman had been faultless in her predictions.

Peter Rhodes, Samantha's devoted husband, leant across and embraced her. "I am so proud of you, my love. See you shortly." He then faced H G with a serious expression. "I hope you are right about this, this woman means everything to me."

H G scoffed. "Stop worrying. We'll be back soon. Are you ready for your task?"

"I am." He stepped back and moved toward the generator switch as H G pulled down the transparent capsule of the machine, enclosing them both inside.

H G knew what they were about to do was highly speculative and extremely dangerous, despite their most rigorous preparations. They were sitting in the prototype of their time-travelling machine, and it was hooked up to the strongest electric generator of their age. But even more importantly, a giant lightning rod was about to be raised into the sky above their building. They were in the midst of a fierce electrical storm, as planned, which would give their machine a boost of energy from a thunderbolt that should launch them into the future. How far into the future was the great unknown, but hopefully they would arrive at a time where a much more powerful energy source than electricity would be available.

Theoretically, the prototype could only move forward in time, but not in space. This meant that no matter what year they travelled to, they would always arrive at the same place, the Rhodes's mansion. However, with a far greater energy source, they believed they had the technical know-how to construct a space-time machine that could take them to whenever and wherever they wanted. That was their aim, their reason for their venture into the future. And if all went well, they would return within a few minutes, sitting together inside their brand-new machine.

They were taking a huge risk, though. They had never actually tested the machine. How could they, without the added lightning bolt? Consequently, they had no idea whether it would work or how far it would take them, or indeed if they would ever be able to return — and even more importantly, if they could actually survive the event.

H G considered herself a lady well ahead of her time. Her family had lacked the funds to send her to Oxford, but as a brilliant student, and due to her academic achievements, she had been granted a full scholarship. She had had her choice of courses but rather than choosing Law or Literature — *subjects better suited to someone of your gender* as suggested by the all-male panel who had selected her — she had chosen physics.

That was how she met her best friend, the much-loved champion Oxford athlete, Samantha Rhodes — the only other female studying physics at Oxford at that time. Samantha was more a mathematician than a physicist, H G the reverse. They often put their minds together with their studies, both of them complementary to rather than competing against the other.

Shorter than Samantha, and of medium build with auburn hair and what she considered handsome rather than pretty features, H G treated herself — and her gender — very seriously. Like her friend, she favoured the collar and tie and tailored look of her time. But unlike Samantha, who was a fashion plate, H G viewed her attire as a statement of the rising power of modern womanhood. Her brain was as clever as any man's, and she was determined to prove it.

She and Samantha had maintained their strong friendship after Oxford, with H G residing and working on her various projects in a converted outbuilding at the Rhodes's mansion. The two of them, along with Samantha's husband, Peter, spent many interesting evenings together discussing all types of hypotheses that were emerging at that dynamic time in the world's history. Their favourite of which was time travel.

Samantha had chosen a separate career path than H G. As a stunning beauty and already reasonably famous as *the best female athlete ever at Oxford* — as quoted by the London Times sports editor — she had chosen a public profile, packing out auditoria throughout the United Kingdom with her lectures on the possibility of time travel. She was an outstanding public speaker, so with her good looks and high profile, her manager had experienced no trouble filling the various assembly rooms, due to the high public interest in her subject matter. Samantha, already a rich woman through her family's and her husband's wealth, was becoming famous talking about her and H G's favourite subject.

H G, on the other hand, had continued her studies and work, with Peter and Samantha not only setting her up at their home but also sponsoring her. Their financial support gave her access to all the relevant scientific knowledge and materials she needed to work full time on her passion, the invention of a time machine.

After years of toil, and the assistance of Samantha's mathematical genius—together with direction from her mysterious dowager—she had succeeded. The dowager in question was the person H G had been summoned to meet via the cryptic message she had received some years earlier. The elderly widow had given H G a notebook and a typed list of instructions to follow to ensure her success. The first of which was to use the power of lightning to achieve her aims.

The notes had been the breakthrough she needed. It meant that theoretically she and Sam could travel to any time almost instantly, but only once—that was the limit of their power. With that knowledge, they had come up with their plan to launch themselves into the future and find a greater power source and technical expertise that would significantly enhance their machine. Once there, they would gather advanced scientific intelligence that could only be utilised by someone with exceptional mathematical brilliance, someone exactly like Samantha Rhodes.

As the two of them strapped themselves into their machine, H G looked forward to their adventure, certain of their success due to her confidence in the dowager's journal.

Peter stood in the outbuilding, watching his precious wife, Samantha, and her great friend, H G, as the airtight capsule was lowered, then they each waved and smiled at him. He wished Samantha wasn't taking such a risk, but he knew there was nothing he could do or say that would keep her from her journey—a journey she and H G had planned for years. They were both strong-willed, modern women who believed in themselves—something he encouraged in Samantha, indeed one of the reasons he loved her so much. He held his tears back and smiled as he waved back at them, determined not to spoil Sam's moment of triumph. She knew he loved her, as she loved him. If he never saw her again, so be it. She was living the life she wanted, and to both women, this was the most important thing a person could do.

H G signalled to him to pull down the switch of the generator, which he did. He watched with amazement as the machine revved up, its image shimmering, then alternately disappearing and reappearing before his eyes. Then it happened. A booming noise erupted as a thunderbolt hit the lightning rod above, and instantly the machine and the girls disappeared.

Peter's true moment of tension had arrived. *Will I ever see them again?* He understood the vagaries of time travel enough to know that Samantha and H G could appear back at any moment, regardless of the amount of time they had spent away.

But they did not come back at once, as they had predicted. Peter paced the floor anxiously as he awaited their return. *What have I done? I should never have agreed to this.* The thought of losing his beloved was tearing him to pieces as he contemplated a life without Samantha, his one, his only, love.

A full hour must have passed, the thunderstorm subsiding as Peter finally sat down, crestfallen and saddened beyond belief. A heartfelt tear trickled down his cheek as he thought of his darling Samantha, trapped somewhere in the vortex of time alongside her friend. He tried to console himself. *At least she died doing what she wanted.*

Then, to his utter amazement and absolute pleasure, a forceful, whirring sound entered the room followed by a bright light and a surge of air that pushed against his brow as slowly an object appeared. *What on Earth?* Before him stood a cylindrical red brick pillar letterbox, about seven-foot high with a five-foot diameter.

The front of the box opened, and H G, only H G, stepped out.

"Where is Samantha?" Peter was horrified.

"I imagine she'll be along presently, in the main residence."

"What do you mean?" He put his head inside the door of the letterbox and was shocked. It was enormous, but more importantly, there was no Samantha. Putting aside his astonishment at the inner dimensions of the box, Peter turned back to H G with alarm. "I don't understand. What's going on?"

"I dematerialised her."

"You what?"

"Relax. I am referring to Samantha Mark Two. Samantha and I both agreed that it was the best thing for her because of the mathematical knowledge she had acquired. Knowledge that was not meant to be known at this time in history."

"But what about you? You've come back."

"Yes, but I have not the slightest knowledge of what Sam was up to. The volume of the equations she wrote on that whiteboard—they have whiteboards in the future, not blackboards—was immense. She came up with this design after seeing several different science fiction programs. It has no Royal cipher, so it is appropriate for any era or any country."

"*Science* fiction? What in heaven's name is that?"

"It's a future literary genre. But that's beside the point. The name of our machine is the DEMAT, short for dematerialisation, the process needed to facilitate space-time travel."

To say Peter was shocked would be a grave understatement. "What is going on H G? Sam's not here and the vastness of those inner dimensions . . . that's just impossible."

"I know, it's amazing, isn't it? The science to create the different interior and exterior dimensions is relativistic, a concept I understood but could never in my wildest dreams formulate. However, Sam could. She's a marvel. That's the reason why that particular Samantha is not here. We will only see the previous version of Sam, and she is, of course, completely unaware of all of this."

"But couldn't we simply explain the situation to her?"

H G's eyes opened wide. "Good Lord, no. That would go against the dowager's instructions. It is vital that Samantha remains ignorant of the machine and all that has happened until a later point in time. Then I will inform her, on this you have my word."

"Dowager?" This was the first time he had heard of such a person. "What has some wealthy widow got to do with all of this?"

"She is the person who has been guiding Sam and me throughout our journey, the reason for our success. But don't concern yourself with that. The most important thing is that you go along with me. You must trust me on this."

Although perplexed, Peter understood the gist of H G's argument. Plus, he trusted her, aware of her great affection for Samantha and genuine care for her welfare. "All right, I will comply with your wishes, but where in blazes is she?"

"I would imagine she is about to walk through the front door of the mansion at any moment. I rang her earlier today from another location, which I travelled to in the DEMAT, diverting and delaying her. It also gave me a chance to test the DEMAT in another position within this time frame, which explains the lateness of my own return here. I had to ensure that I did not overlap my entries. Otherwise, I may well have dematerialised the DEMAT."

Peter had no idea what H G meant by all that, but before he could query her, she continued with her discourse.

"Remember, Peter. This Samantha we will soon see is the one that existed before our time travel. She will be completely unaware of what has happened. This is vitally important. I will explain it all to you in due course but please, follow my lead for now."

They left the outbuilding and headed for the mansion.

Once inside the main parlour, as if on cue, H G heard the front door open, and after a few short moments, Samantha walked into the room, as stunning as ever, wearing the same suit and bonnet she had worn when they had left in the machine.

"Hello, my darling." She crossed the room and kissed Peter on the lips before acknowledging H G with a smile. "H G, rotten luck about the delay, have you fixed the problem with the machine?"

"I have. Not to worry, thunderstorms are predicted for tomorrow evening so we will have only been delayed a day, nothing at all in the scheme of things."

"It certainly was quite a storm. But it was so peaceful afterwards, which is why I walked home." Samantha passed H G a small book, *Shares and Property movements from 1885-1895*. "Here is the volume you asked me to collect from the library. Whatever would you want with that?"

"It's not for me, it's for a friend."

Samantha barely acknowledged H G's answer seemingly preoccupied with something else as she took off her bonnet and gloves. "The strangest thing happened to me on my walk home."

H G immediately perked. "Oh yes, what was that?"

"I took a short cut through a back street, which was completely deserted, and all at once I felt a presence behind me, accompanied by the coldest of feelings."

"What was it?"

"Nothing. I turned around, and there was no one there. But that feeling, it was unearthly, as though someone had walked over my grave." Samantha shook herself. "But something else happened that was very strange. A tall man wearing a cloak and a broad brim hat appeared from the shadows some twenty or so yards away. He was holding a small device. It appeared to be a camera of some sort. I tried to get a look at his face, but he walked past me before I could."

Peter panicked. "Good Lord, are you okay?"

Samantha turned and smiled at him as she placed her hat and gloves on the bench. "Of course, I am, why wouldn't I be? He had no ill intent, and as for the feeling, we have all felt such feelings before, haven't we?"

"I certainly haven't," Peter said.

"Well, I have," H G admitted. "Several times. It is very spooky when it happens."

"You two women, so in touch with your mystical souls."

H G was delighted by what Samantha had experienced. *Everything is going to plan.* She quickly changed the topic. "What have you both got planned for tomorrow, during the day?"

"I am vetting applications for my next group of admissions, so I will be very busy," Peter replied.

"And I have a lecture at the Masonic Hall. I should be home about six."

H G smiled. "Perfect, we shall all meet in the outbuilding then. What an evening it should be. Our time-travel adventure finally on its way."

"Indeed, I can't wait." Samantha shivered with excitement. "Are you dining with us tonight, H G?"

"Not tonight, there are still some things I need to go over with regards to our machine. I shall see you tomorrow around six." She leant across and kissed Samantha on the cheek, then left the room.

Peter followed her out, excusing himself beforehand. "I will be back shortly, darling, there is something I need to discuss with H G."

He caught up with her quickly. "Are you certain of what you are doing? I feel so guilty deceiving Samantha."

Her mind held no doubts. "Absolutely, you will see. Remember, this deception is what *she* asked for."

"Okay then. But I will hold you to your word that you will eventually inform Samantha of what truly happened." Peter leant across and kissed her on the cheek. "Good night, H G." He went back into the main residence, seemingly comfortable about their hidden arrangement.

H G was sure in her actions. Her mysterious dowager had got them this far without incident, tomorrow setting in train events that would put them all on their predestined paths.

CHAPTER TWO

Melbourne 2018

Shane Courtney followed the prison guard to the visitor's centre, intrigued by his surprise visitor. *Peter Rhodes? I've never heard of the guy.* Still, it was a welcome break from his daily laundry duties. He and his foster brother, Simon Lewis, had been sentenced to life imprisonment without parole for murder, fraud, and the creation of a white slavery racket in their home city of Melbourne. With their reputation preceding them, they had soon become a respected pair within their new community. Simon's psychotic mind adding the necessary element of fear to their standing.

Shane was taken to a table where he was greeted by a tall, elegant, clean-shaven man in his thirties, dressed entirely in black. The man stood and smiled, offering his hand, which Shane shook before they both sat down.

"So, Peter Rhodes, who in the fuck are you? And what is this all about?"

"What I am about to tell you, Mr Courtney, will shock you beyond belief." The guy spoke with an upper-class English accent, his vowels rounded and his consonants sharp.

"I doubt that very much."

"I have been sent here to take you to London. It appears your presence is vital if I am to rescue my wife."

What the fuck? My presence? I'm in here for life. This bloke's a nutter. "Is that right, mate? And how do you propose to achieve that?"

"Don't worry about that, it has all been arranged. You're to be smuggled out in a laundry basket."

Suddenly Shane's interest was piqued. He had no idea who this silly bastard was or what perceived part Shane was meant to play. But if the guy could get him out of here, he would go anywhere and do anything. "Go on."

"When you have finished your duties today, a guard will facilitate your rescue. Do exactly as he tells you, and you will be free to assist us in our hour of need."

Facilitate? Hour of Need? Who in the fucking hell talks like that? And as for assisting him, fuck that. As soon as he, and Simon—for he was going nowhere without him—were free, they would be fucking off. He had a stash hidden away.

His visitor appeared to be reading his mind. "And do not think that you and your compatriot will be free to abscond."

Shane was taken aback.

"Yes, I know about your psychotic foster brother. But as I said, do not think the two of you will be running off somewhere with one of your elaborate schemes in mind. Before you are placed into the basket, you will be shackled in transport restraints, hand and foot. You will be doing exactly as we tell you."

Fuck, this bastard's a psychic. "We? Who in the fuck is *we*?"

"Myself, and H G."

"H G? You mean H. G. Wells?" *Got that wrong, he's not a psychic, he's a psycho.*

"The one and the same."

Jesus, this bloke is fucked. "So, did he bring his time machine?"

"It's *she* actually, her name is Hope Grace. And of course, how else do you think we got here from the nineteenth century?"

Given any other situation Shane would have got up and walked away, but he was a captive audience, in more ways than one. Even if the bloke was a raving lunatic, the guy was promising to get him and his foster brother out of prison. With that in mind, he decided to play along, humour him.

"Okay, so what do we have to do?"

"Nothing. Just carry on as normal, then at the end of your shift, the guard will tell you to stay behind. That is when he will restrain you both and hide you in the basket."

"Someone will check the basket."

"That's all been taken care of. Oh, and another thing, an added incentive if you like. The woman we have to rescue, Samantha Rhodes, is your great-great-grandmother. So if you are unsuccessful in your mission, you will cease to exist."

This was all too much for Shane's pragmatic soul. "Don't be so fucking stupid. How in the fuck do you expect me to believe all this?"

"I don't. You are far too much the realist, much like your great-great-grandmother. But if and when you are standing in nineteenth-century London, perhaps then you will be convinced. Wouldn't you agree?"

Shane studied his visitor. As one of the world's greatest charlatans, he was an expert at reading people, especially their deceit, but in this man, he could not detect any such signs. Either this Peter Rhodes—possibly his own great-great-grandfather—was a complete lunatic, or he was telling the truth. Either way, Shane would find out later that day.

He stood up and shook Peter's hand. "Thanks for the visit, Mr Rhodes. Even if you are as insane as I think you are, it's been an interesting interlude from my eternal drudgery. And if you are not, I shall see you soon."

Peter shook his hand and smiled. "Myself, and H G, she'll be there too."

"Of course, she will. See you, mate." With that he turned and left his bizarre visitor, wondering how he was going to explain all of this to his psychotic foster brother. *He will probably understand it better than me.*

The front doorbell of Jennifer Best's delightful St Kilda residence rang. Its sharp tone shaking her from her reverie as she lazed on her couch. She had purchased the home, a stately Victorian terrace nestled behind shady trees in a secluded cul-de-sac, courtesy of the proceeds from her worldwide bestseller. The story of her incredible, life-saving adventure that had resulted in shattering a white slavery ring and the arrest of its mastermind, Shane Courtney, along with his murderous henchman, Simon Lewis, had proved to be a runaway success, turning her into a multi-millionaire.

She still shuddered when she thought of Shane and his duplicitous mind and how much she had loved him. *How did I ever fall for such bullshit?* "Daria, can you get that?"

Daria had been with her ever since her rescue from Shane's murderous cult by Jennifer, the Police Minister, Susan Turnbull, and the now Inspector, Rebecca Browning, who had become one of Jennifer and Daria's best friends. For the last two years, Daria had been studying martial arts with a passion, becoming an expert in her chosen skill, karate.

Daria walked past the large opened door of Jennifer's living room wearing her karate uniform, wiping the sweat from her face with a towel. "Sure thing, babe."

Jennifer loved Daria's carefree, fearless attitude, but even more so her dedication to her craft. True to the vow she had made after her rescue, Daria had turned herself into a lethal fighting machine, determined never again to become the slave of another. She was the perfect bodyguard and assistant for Jennifer's alter ego Heather West—the intrepid investigative reporter—and they had become inseparable allies.

Daria returned with a young lady who appeared to be in her mid-twenties. The woman was wearing a single-breasted suit with a floor-length, elegantly draped skirt together with an upturned collar and tie, and bonnet. *I love her clothes.*

"Heather" — Daria was using Jen's nom de plume — "this is H G Wells. Apparently, she has a story of extreme interest."

Jennifer examined the woman in disbelief. "H G Wells?"

The young lady smiled. "I am, but not the H G you are alluding to. He is the other H G, as I like to call him, my elder cousin. My name is Hope Grace Wells. But please, call me H G."

She spoke with a refined English accent. Jennifer was intrigued. *A cousin of Herbert George Wells? Hardly.* "Please come in Ms Wells, and take a seat."

The young lady continued to smile warmly as she sat in one of Jennifer's comfortable lounge chairs. "*Mizz,* I love the terminology of your times. It must be so liberating to not be labelled by your title."

Your times? Once again Jennifer was puzzled. "What have you got for us H G?"

Leaning forward in her chair, H G studied Jennifer before answering. "A young lady of great significance and very dear to us all has been kidnapped."

This is beginning to sound interesting. "Then why don't you go to the police? I am a journalist, not a detective."

"We will be bringing a police presence into these matters presently. However, my client gave me strict instructions to first seek you and your assistant out."

My assistant? No one knows anything about Daria or our fledgling relationship. Jennifer was beginning to feel uncomfortable. The young lady was dressed in nineteenth-century clothes, just as Shane's sect members had been. *Surely, he's not involved? That's impossible, he's locked away for life with his crazy foster brother.*

Daria intervened. "H. G. Wells? Didn't he write something about a time machine?"

"He wrote about it, then I invented it a few years afterwards. With the help of the woman we are about to rescue, my best friend, Samantha."

Jennifer was bemused, amused, and startled all at once. "You built a time machine?"

"I did, with the mathematical assistance of Samantha who is a genius in such matters. It was a rather rudimentary device, able to travel forward in time, but not space. After it was built, Samantha and I travelled to the future to modernise it, leaving the old one in the other H G's museum and then returning in the new model. That was two days ago. Yesterday Samantha's husband, Peter, also a good friend who you will meet presently, advised me that she had been kidnapped. And I believe it has something to do with our machine."

She seems so genuine. But this can't be real. "H G, as much as your story sounds interesting, I fail to see how Daria and I can be of assistance."

Daria tilted her head and squinted her eyes. "Are you following this, Jen?" Her hand went to her mouth, instantly realising she had just revealed Jennifer's true identity.

"It's all right, Daria," H G reassured her. "I know that Heather West is actually Jennifer Best. In fact, I know quite a good deal about you both. In particular, your rescue and your dedication to becoming the person that stands before us today. You are to be congratulated."

Daria sat up straighter with a smile, obviously chuffed.

H G then turned to Jennifer, once again smiling. "And you, madam, are of even greater import, your participation extremely vital to our mission's success."

Despite the surrealism of their situation, Jennifer was completely enthralled by this strange, fascinating woman—a supposed time traveller. "Your information about us, how did you come by it?"

"My intelligence comes from a wealthy dowager who somehow is aware of all of our destinies. For example, she had knowledge of my time machine well before it was built, and everything she has since told me has come to pass. Consequently, I have absolute confidence in her veracity."

Veracity? She certainly speaks and sounds like someone from the nineteenth century. Jennifer was fascinated. *What a story, what an adventure. If only it were true.* However, due to her recent history involving Shane Courtney, her cynical side needed absolute proof.

Jennifer's visitor must have sensed her unease. "Allow me, Miss Best. I can see you remain uncertain. Let me reveal a few of your own idiosyncrasies of which only your closest friends would be aware."

Jennifer smiled nervously, not particularly comfortable with where the conversation was heading.

"Firstly, your fetish for tailored clothing, your present attire of a business suit while relaxing at home a perfect example."

Jennifer felt utterly exposed, her cheeks were on fire. She looked across at Daria who was staring at her, grinning. Jennifer turned back to H G, trying her best to appear confident, authoritative. "It is not a fetish, more a penchant."

Naturally, Daria contradicted her. "Fetish is spot on, she loves wearing tailored clothes."

Jennifer could have killed her. "This is all a bit personal, could we change the subject?"

H G smiled. "I don't know why you are so embarrassed. In the world where I come from, as you can see"—she looked down at her own outfit, flourishing her hands—"all the ladies wear such attire, our clothes made by men's tailors."

Daria piped up again, grinning. "Jen would love that."

"Daria, stop it, you're becoming annoying."

H G spoke again. "However, the one thing we have to

endure that you do not is tight corsetry."

"It sounds like your own personal paradise, Jen." Daria continued her teasing.

Jennifer was about to respond, furious at her mischievous friend, when H G started laughing, her hilarity becoming infectious. Soon she was laughing, too, as was Daria.

The laughter eventually settled down, but not before Jennifer recalled the warm feeling she had experienced between her legs when H G had mentioned the tight corsets. *For Christ's sake, girl, get a grip on yourself.*

She composed herself, cleared her throat, trying to sound as unaffected as possible. "As humorous as all that was, it should be noted that all this embarrassing information could have been garnered from my ill-advised appearance on that tailor's website. What else do you have?"

H G continued to smile. "Oh, I have encyclopaedic knowledge at my fingertips, Miss Best, if you so desire. Now let's see." She sat back in the chair, her elbows on the armrest, her gloved hands together at her lips as if she were in deep thought. "You first made love to Shane Courtney—"

"Whoa!" Horrified, Jennifer held up her hand to interrupt. *Christ, how could she know this stuff? Unless, of course, Shane was behind it all.* She decided to go along with it, for now, frightened that other more personal, more embarrassing details of her sexual idiosyncrasies may emerge. "That's enough. I am convinced. The fact that you are even aware of this event adds to my eternal shame."

"Don't be too hard on yourself, Miss Best. It is of my understanding that he, too, was deeply in love with you."

"I suppose, in his own twisted way, he could have been. But we are off the subject. What is it that Daria and I are meant to do? The sooner it is done the sooner I can return and start writing my next best seller. That is if what you are telling me is true."

"You will both be coming with me, all corseted up in your

Victorian finery. Welcome to eighteen-ninety-eight London society, ladies."

Daria rubbed her hands together, obviously delighted with the prospect. As for Jennifer, the thought of her body being subjected to tight Victorian corsetry and tailoring once again caused a feeling of warmth to spread through her nether regions—the embarrassing development, fortunately, hidden from her companion's awareness.

The doorbell rang again. Daria answered it and returned with a familiar figure, Inspector Rebecca Browning, who walked into the room accompanied by a tall, rather handsome gentleman dressed in black.

Jennifer was surprised and happy to see her good friend again. "Rebecca, what brings you here?"

"Mr Rhodes here has convinced me that you ladies need me. I understand we are about to embark on a brief adventure."

Brief? I would hardly call it that. We're all about to be transposed to eighteen-ninety-eight London. "But what about your work, won't they miss you?"

"I'm sure they can handle me being away for a few hours."

"A few hours?" Jennifer frowned. "We're going to London."

Rebecca's eyes opened wide, and she turned to her tall companion. "I thought you said it would only take a short while, Mr Rhodes?"

H G intervened. "Less if you prefer, Miss Browning. Allow me to explain, my name is Wells, H G Wells."

"Of time machine fame? But he's a man."

"That's the other H G. I am Hope Grace, his younger cousin. I, along with my dearest friend and colleague—Peter's wife, Samantha, the kidnapped woman—actually built the machine. He only wrote about it, the poor darling."

With her mouth agape, Rebecca appeared absolutely flabbergasted.

H G chuckled. "The small adventure of which you speak is one of time travel, and as such, we can have you back a minute after we leave if you so desire."

Rebecca, the most pragmatic of souls and clearly astounded by all she was hearing, turned to Daria with an expression that pleaded for some sanity.

Daria grinned. "I can hardly wait."

Rebecca immediately turned back to Jennifer who, sensing her bewilderment, tried to reassure her. "I know it sounds completely far-fetched Rebecca, but H G knows things about me that she could not possibly know."

"What sort of things?"

Jennifer was about to answer, but once again Daria intervened, her amusement evident. "Things like her fetish for tailored clothing for starters."

Rebecca gasped. "Her what?"

Jennifer glared at Daria who smiled back innocently, clearly enjoying herself. "Don't worry about it, the detail is not important. The main thing is that she has convinced me. I mean how else could H. G. Wells' younger cousin get here, other than by time travel?"

"Jen, darling, surely you're not going along with all this crap?" Rebecca asked.

"I know it seems like absolute bullshit, Becky, but we'll soon know, won't we? If we hop in her machine and it takes us nowhere, then clearly it is all crap, as you say."

Jennifer's reasoning seemed to satisfy Rebecca. "Fair enough." She then turned to H G. "So, what do we do now?"

"The first thing we have to do is get you girls changed into appropriate attire. Peter, could you get the trunk from the DEMAT?"

Jennifer frowned, puzzled as Peter headed toward her back garden. "The time machine? It's here?"

"It certainly is, on your back lawn as a matter of fact."

Jennifer headed toward her back garden with Daria, Rebecca, and H G following behind. She could not believe what she saw in front of her. It was an old style, cylindrical letter-box. "Hold on, this is nothing like the time machine that H G — the other H G that is — depicts in his novel."

"When Samantha and I were in the year twenty-seventy-eight we made a few changes, modernised it. The prototype was only a time machine. This, however, takes us through both time and space."

"How in the bloody hell are we all supposed to fit in that?" Daria blurted.

H G frowned. "You Australian women curse a good deal, don't you?"

Before Daria could respond to the surprising statement, H G pressed on. "My question was rhetorical, Daria. Yours, however, is quite relevant. Indeed, it was the very first problem I asked Samantha to solve when first we came across the concept."

She paused and took a deep breath, gaining an utterly rapt audience. "Allow me to explain. The machine is dimensionally transcendental, that is, its interior exists in a different relativistic dimension to its exterior. When you get inside, you'll see. We named it the DEMAT, short for dematerialisation."

Daria stared at H G, captivated. "Twenty-seventy-eight? Wow, what was it like?"

"Not much different to your present time. But we were in London, not Melbourne, so I can't be precise. For example, your delightful cable cars that I saw go by at the end of your cul-de-sac. I have no idea if they still exist. We were on the internet and in our London home most of the time."

Rebecca glared as though she had H G trapped in the middle of an interrogation. "If you can go back in time, then why don't you just go back to a time before Samantha was kidnapped, instead of going through all this rigmarole?"

"Great question, one I would expect a clever detective such as yourself would ask. It seems our dowager was correct about you."

"Dowager?" Rebecca asked in a baffled tone.

"A wealthy widow."

"I know what a dowager is. But how could she know about me?"

"She knows a good deal about all of us. But back to your question, why don't we go back and change what has already happened? According to the dowager, the answer is elementary. What has occurred is predestined. It is meant to occur, written into the fabric of space-time. Samantha's abduction must be allowed to transpire so that all of our destinies, including hers, will be fulfilled."

Jennifer was as bewildered as Rebecca. "So all this is happening for a purpose?"

"Absolutely, and in a precise, calculated manner."

"Precise? Calculated? What do you mean by that?" Rebecca asked.

"One of the basic tenets of time travel is that no one can be in the same place at the same time as their previous incarnation. Therefore, if you are travelling back in time and reappear while in the presence of your former self, your second incarnation, that is the time traveller, will instantly dematerialise, or disappear if you prefer."

"So that means that you must always arrive back after you have left?"

"Exactly. Unless it is your intention for the second version of yourself to be dematerialised."

Daria intervened with her own question. "What happens if you travel forward in time and you are already there?"

"But you can't *already be there*. You must have travelled

back in time from that future moment, for you to be leaving from the past."

Jennifer completely understood, whereas Daria continued to look flummoxed. "Don't worry, Daria, I will explain it to you later."

"No, you won't. I've had enough time-travel talk to last a lifetime."

Everybody laughed at this, including Daria.

Peter came out from within the DEMAT, dragging a large trunk behind him. "Corset and tailored costume time, ladies. You are about to become Victorian gentlewomen."

Jennifer felt the warmth below her waist instantly reappear.

Chapter Three

London 1898

Samantha slowly woke, taking in her surrounds as she did. The last thing she remembered was walking along a back street on her way home after giving a lecture on the possibility of time travel at the Masonic Hall. She had been in high spirits, thinking of her upcoming journey with H G that evening in their time machine, looking forward to their risky but exciting adventure.

As she walked past a black carriage, a masked man had leapt out and snatched her, throwing her into the carriage before placing a cloth over her mouth and nose, forcing her to breathe in a toxic substance that sent her into a state of unconsciousness. She remembered how tenaciously she had struggled and how terrified she had been, and how all she could think of at the time was her darling husband, Peter.

As she slowly regained her senses, she realised she was bound and gagged, lying on a thin mattress in a dingy room, which was illuminated by a small light globe that hung from the ceiling. There was a stairwell leading upwards, so she presumed the room was below the ground, perhaps some sort of cellar.

She was bound exactly as her then soon-to-be husband, Doctor Peter Rhodes, had tied for her for her admission to his clinic, The Institute of Female Behaviour, years before. It was there he had not only cured her melancholy by revealing her libido to her — a method he used to cure all his patients—but where they had also fallen in love, marrying a short time thereafter. Their marriage was one of pure bliss. Peter's eagerness to see his beautiful wife bound in her tailored finery corresponding perfectly with Samantha's own furtive desire for it to occur.

Her current bondage, however, though physically the same, was doing no such thing for her libido. No love surrounded the act. Her bonds were not an expression of another's affection, but an act of violence and aggression, simply because it was against her will.

She remembered looking up the word *violence* in her dictionary just two days prior, searching for some rationalisation for her oh so different desires. It had read, *Violence: behaviour involving physical force intended to hurt, damage, or kill someone or something.* She remembered thinking at the time that the definition was incomplete, that the words *against their will* should be added. Her current circumstances both clarified and reinforced her thoughts.

Her legs were bound at the knees over her dress, causing it to billow out while her ankles were also tied tightly over her boots beneath her dress, her arms bound behind her and trussed to her body—exactly the same circumstance that had awoken her sensuality that very first day with Peter.

Samantha struggled from her side, sitting up on the mattress before looking at herself in the dirty mirror on the opposite wall. She was wearing her azure walking suit and bonnet, her favourite outfit. Some type of fabric filled her mouth, which had been tightly wrapped and secured with a medical bandage, silencing her. Her mouth was dry, while a tinge of a headache from the toxic chemical she had been forced to inhale, lingered. Looking around for some hint of escape, she could see it was hopeless. She was fixed here for as long as her captors wanted.

But why have I been abducted, and who is behind it? She knew Peter had his critics amongst the medical fraternity. His faultless results often showing them up in the worst of lights. But surely this was taking matters too far?

Perhaps she had been taken because of her own actions? As a public figure and one of the nation's leading physicists—and a female to boot—her success had put many a chauvinistic male scientist's noses out of joint. But again, she couldn't imagine her academic enemies resorting to such tactics.

She moved back onto the mattress lying on her side making herself as comfortable as possible when the door above the stairs opened. A tall, cloaked man of slim build entered, his face hidden behind a mask, his clothes the mark of a successful man.

He looked directly at her eyes as he knelt and undid her gag. "I am dreadfully sorry about this, Mrs Rhodes, but I could see no alternative." He spoke with a resonant tone, his voice powerful and, even more importantly from Samantha's present viewpoint, memorable.

Samantha spat the rag out of her mouth as he sat her up. "How dare you treat me so? I am outraged. Do you think such deeds will go unpunished?"

He chuckled as he sat on the mattress beside her, wrapping his unwelcome arm around her trussed torso. "Oh, they will indeed go unpunished, dear lady." His covered face was nearly touching hers. "And you, Mrs Rhodes, will be back in your nice home as soon as you tell me what you know about Mr Wells and his letterbox time machine."

Letterbox? What was he talking about? Samantha shrugged his arm away as best she could, her expressed disapproval causing him to cease his embrace. "I presume you are talking about H. G. Wells. I have only met the man on a few occasions. And as for the letterbox time machine, I have no idea what you are talking about." This was the truth. She had helped *her* H G invent her time machine, a secret shared between Peter, H G, and herself. But that machine was in the style as described in H G's famous cousin's book, nothing at all like a letterbox.

"Is that the way it's going to be?" He stood up and walked across to a sink and poured some water into a glass, returning with it. "Here, have a drink. I am sure you need it."

Samantha swallowed the water gratefully. She was parched and had no idea how long she had been there.

Once she finished drinking, he resumed his conversation. "As soon as you have answered all of my questions you will be allowed to leave."

Samantha remained puzzled. "And what makes you think I would ever answer you, after being in receipt of such brutal behaviour?"

"Oh, you will answer me, Mrs Rhodes, believe me. We have ways of making you talk."

Samantha held back her laughter at his melodramatic statement. "Don't be ridiculous. Do you plan to torture me? And talk about what? What is it that you want from me?"

"Information about your travels into the future with Mr Wells, where I imagine he developed his latest time machine, the letterbox version I speak of."

Samantha could not help herself and immediately started laughing. "Mr Wells and I, travelling to the future? In a letterbox?" She spoke between gasps, spluttering her words. "As I said before . . . I have no idea what you are talking about."

He smiled at her with a sly expression. "Haven't you now? Then how do you explain this?"

He pulled a series of small, square, black and white photographs from an envelope. The first one was of a large, cylindrical letterbox standing on the footpath of a London street.

Samantha had seen many such structures. Thus she was unimpressed. "So?"

"Be patient."

The next photograph showed the front of the box opening and a woman exiting it, her face obscured, while the one after that was of the same woman moving into the shadows nearby.

"Keep watching." He laid out the remaining photos.

To Samantha's utter astonishment the next frame was of her, wearing her double-breasted suit and walking toward the camera, passing the same shadows where the woman had gone. The letterbox was no longer there. *What on Earth?*

Samantha's bafflement grew as she viewed the remaining sequence of events laid out before her. She was still walking toward the camera, while the other woman had emerged from the shadows and was now directly behind her. In the next frame, only Samantha was visible, her face turned behind her as if she was looking for the woman, who had disappeared.

Her heart skipped a beat, and a chill ran up her spine. *I know when this happened. It was yesterday when I was walking home from the library after the storm. That was the eerie, chilling feeling. And it was a camera that the man in the cloak was holding.* But as for the mysterious woman and the letterbox, she had no idea.

"Clearly this is some sort of forgery," she said, giving her confused mind some time to comprehend what she had just viewed.

"There is no forgery here, madam. They are my very own photographs, taken by myself yesterday."

Samantha was utterly perplexed. She had no memory of the letterbox, or time machine if that's what it was. Her rational brain searched for a solution. The clue was the woman from the shadows. *Is it possible?* H G had told her what would happen if ever such a circumstance should occur—

the second version of the person dematerialising. *Could the woman from the shadows be me? Is this what happened?* Had she, in fact, travelled to the future with H G, then returned to a moment in time before they had left, causing her second self to dematerialise? *But why?* It didn't make sense.

Her captor brought her musing back to the present.

"Well, Mrs Rhodes, what do you make of it all?"

She had no intention of telling him anything, especially about H G, who, unlike the other H. G. Wells and herself, was not a public figure. "I am sorry, but I am at a loss to explain it."

He scanned Samantha's face, his gaze flitting from side to side beneath the mask as if he was searching for signs of deception. "Mmm. We shall soon see. I have a machine, a recent invention called a polygraph. Submit yourself to that, and if it shows you are truthful, then you will be free to leave."

"Truly? Free to leave?"

"I give you my word as a gentleman and a scholar."

Gentleman? I hardly think so. Still, what do I have to lose? "Fine, let's get on with it so I can get back home to my husband and my work."

Graham Jenkins was an industrialist, a captain of industry who had made his fortune in manufacturing. He had become obsessed with the concept of time travel ever since reading H. G. Wells's novel some three years ago. The book was so detailed with its description of the machine Graham had become convinced of its existence.

Then, just the morning before, he had received a package that contained the strangest of cameras that developed the photos immediately after they were taken. With it came a typed note showing him how to use the device and informing him that the film — the last of its kind — had only six photos left on it. The first of these was to be used to familiarise himself with the camera's operation, the remainder to be used on Mrs Samantha Rhodes at a certain time and place later that day. The rest of the letter was rather cryptic, suggesting that his time machine questions would all be answered by the resultant photos.

What he saw was why he had arranged to have Mrs Rhodes abducted, although her brutal treatment by the thug he had hired was more than he had bargained for.

He untied her, moved her to a chair, and attached the wires of the latest scientific marvel, a polygraph, or lie detector as it was more commonly known.

He asked the first question to test her reaction. "Is your name Samantha Rhodes?"

"Yes"

He watched the path of the marker and saw no substantial movement.

"Are you in love with your husband?"

"Yes."

Again, there was no pronounced movement. He continued asking the obvious questions for a few moments, and Mrs Rhodes tested negatively for them all. Then he sprung the important question.

"Have you ever been in Mr Well's time machine?"

"No."

The result was the same.

He fired off the next few questions rapidly.

"Have you ever time travelled?"

"No."

"Have you any knowledge of a letterbox time machine?"

"No."

He proceeded with additional pointed questions relating to the letterbox. All of which were met with a definitive, unambiguous reply that caused the machine to barely ripple.

Clearly, she was telling the truth, even though the photos showed otherwise. He was wasting his time with her. He needed to speak with H. G. Wells himself.

Unbuckling her from the machine he took her over to the mattress, taking the rope.

She looked at him with horror. "You are not going to bind me again?"

"Of course not, I am not a thug."

He went across to the wardrobe, depositing the rope before grabbing a chain with a shackle and some padlocks and walking back to her. "Sit down."

She looked around as if she was thinking of escape. "Don't be stupid. I still have the rope, which I won't hesitate to use if you are foolish."

She sighed, sat, and watched as he applied the shackle to her leg immediately above her boot, tightening it before locking it. He then padlocked a chain to it and then to a ring in the concrete wall. "It is about fifteen yards long. You won't be able to reach the stairs, but you will be able to reach the sink for water to drink and wash, and be able to use the toilet. There is some canned food in the wardrobe and an opener so you should be fine."

He stood as Mrs Rhodes looked at him with fear written all over her face. "You are not going to leave me here?"

"I have no alternative. But don't worry I have left enough bread crumbs for your husband to find you. How long that takes is up to him. It could be a few days or a few weeks, but regardless, you have enough food to last." He chuckled as he walked toward the stairs. "Unless it takes him a year of course, then you will be in trouble."

She stood, attempting to follow him but her tether stopped her just short of the stairwell. He opened the cellar door at the top of the stairs and then looked back at her. Tears rolled down her attractive face, which was wrung with desperation as she pleaded with him.

"Please, kind sir, have pity on me. Don't leave me here all alone."

"Goodbye, Mrs Rhodes. Perhaps we'll meet again some-day." With that, he turned and walked through the door, locking it behind him. The thick wooden portal silencing her anguished cries for mercy.

Melbourne 2018

Rebecca had found it hard to comprehend the massive size of the interior of the DEMAT when she had first entered the letterbox, but after a few moments, her doubts of possible time travel faded.

She and Jennifer had laughed at each other when they had put on their corsets. Daria had decided not to wear one—her skinny, athletic frame with her tiny bosom making it entirely unnecessary. Besides she had worn one for years while a slave at Shane's sect, so she had no particular desire to ever wear one again. Daria's outfit was a full-length, navy blue dress with a tight bodice that was complemented with a cape and bonnet.

Jennifer, on the other hand, seemed to relish her corset, supporting herself against the DEMAT while urging Rebecca to pull the ties with all her might. When Jennifer had finished dressing, she looked every bit the Victorian society lady in her tailored suit that fitted snugly about her now tiny waist, a fashionable bonnet pinned on her blond hair that had been tied up into a chignon, and her face now bereft of makeup, except for some white powder. Her gloved hands held her parasol in front of her as she posed in front of a mirror, pointing the toe of her ankle length, buttoned boot out from under her elegant skirt as she admired herself. Rebecca had to admit Jennifer looked as grand as one could be in her attire.

The only reason Rebecca had agreed to wear a corset, which was tied as loosely as it could be without falling off, was because her ample cleavage required support, and bras did not exist in 1898. Her outfit was much looser than Jennifer's. It appeared H G's dowager was somehow aware of all their preferences. She also wore a bonnet pinned atop her brunette chignon along with gloves and ankle boots but, like Daria, she was without a parasol.

She looked and felt decidedly uncomfortable, her outfit nothing like her normal attire of a pants suit with an open jacket. Thankfully, the looseness of her jacket afforded her enough room to sheathe her shoulder holster and gun, her handcuffs tucked safely away in one of her jacket's pockets. Unlike both Daria and Jennifer, Rebecca was not at all perturbed by the fact that she was not wearing makeup, for her it was normal.

H G locked the door of the DEMAT, sealing it before walking across to the console and setting the coordinates for their journey.

"Off to London?" asked Jennifer.

"Not yet. We have one small pick up along the way."

Jennifer laughed. "Oh yes, anyone we know?"

H G said nothing, merely smiling as she pushed the DEMAT lever forward. The time machine made a whirring sound as it left the scene.

Shane stood with Simon at the end of their shift, both wearing their prison uniforms, and both shackled in transport restraints. Everything had gone as Peter had said it would, except instead of placing them into a laundry basket, the guard had shuffled them over to the furthest corner of the laundry and had told them to wait, before leaving the room.

It had been ten minutes, and Shane was becoming agitated. "Where is the bastard? How in the fuck is he getting us out of here?"

In contrast, Simon was cool and calm. "Relax Shane, all this is meant to happen, so it will."

Shane glared at his foster brother, wondering what in the fuck was going on with him. The day before Simon had asked Shane to knock him on the head so that he would be sent to the infirmary, saying he needed an alibi. That had not particularly surprised him, as Simon was up to all sorts of shenanigans since joining his prison community. And earlier, all afternoon, he had been acting strange — well stranger than normal that is — walking around as though he was certain of his destiny, utterly serene.

He knew of Simon's worship of Jack the Ripper, and how he had memorised all the dates along with the precise locations and the methodology of his hero's bloody murders. Perhaps that was it, as they were supposedly headed back toward those times. Regardless, he had never seen his brother so content, so at peace.

"Stop with this philosophical bullshit, Simon. We are probably just going on a ride in a truck somewhere. Someone out there wants us to do something for them, to use our talents. This is all just some ruse meant to entice us, you'll see."

But Simon remained steadfast, his face rigid, his cold, green eyes focused as if he was staring at something in the distance.

Shane shook his head, fiddling with the connecting chain between his cuffs and manacles. *Poor bastard, he's as mad as they come, but I love him.*

A loud whirring sound erupted before them, the air around them pressed against their faces as a bright light appeared. Shane shielded himself, turning sideways and ducking his head. In contrast, Simon just stood there, his eyes closed against the force that blew across his face.

Once the noise receded, Shane turned his head back. To his utter astonishment, materialising before his eyes was a bloody letterbox. He started laughing, realising some bastard was having a big fat lend of him. Someone had gone to extraordinary lengths to take the piss, to build him up with hopes of escape, then let him down with a humiliating farce. *Well, fuck you whoever you are, I'm not buying.*

Shane could hear some shuffling and then out of the door stepped Peter Rhodes and a young woman dressed in nineteenth-century clothing. Shane started laughing again, uncontrollably, while both visitors looked at him incredulously. His laughter eased just enough for him to say something. "So who in the fuck is this? H. G. Wells?" He doubled over when he saw their expressions, the indignant look on the young woman's face and the continued incredulity of the so-called Peter Rhodes.

Simon walked over and kneed Shane in the thigh, both hurting and shocking him to the same degree. "What the fuck, Simon?"

His foster brother had a fervent, cruel look on his face — a look that scared even Shane — as he spoke between stiff, drawn lips, his piercing green eyes fiercely intent. "Don't fuck this up, Shane. This is very important to me."

What the fuck? Was he falling for this shit? Shane knew a con when he saw one, and this, no matter how elaborately orchestrated, was just that. He would show him. "Okay, okay. Let's go inside this letterbox. Then you'll see what fucking bullshit this is. These bastards are charlatans, no better than us."

Peter Rhodes and the woman stood aside, allowing them to enter the supposed time machine. Once inside, Shane was astounded by what he saw, looking around at the vast space that defied reality. But the disbelief he felt paled when he saw the expression of the blonde woman on the far side of the room.

"What in the fuck is that prick doing here?" she roared.

Jesus Christ, it's Jen. Beautiful, wonderful, foul-mouthed Jen.

CHAPTER FOUR

London 1898

Samantha had settled down, realising that her imprison-ment in this lonely tomb was truly happening, a circum-stance she would have to endure whether she liked it or not. She decided to explore her prison, try and make some sense of her misfortune. The length of her chain allowed her to reach everything, the toilet, the desk, the sink, and the ward-robe. Her situation had been planned to perfection with even the light switch within her reach above her mattress, which thankfully was not as filthy as she first thought. This conces-sion would at least allow her to sleep in darkness.

Opening the wardrobe, she was both surprised and elated by what she saw. There were two fresh blankets neatly fold-ed on one of the shelves along with a clean pillow and sheet for the mattress. But what surprised her most of all were the items hidden in the wardrobe drawers. Fresh, clean, pre-cious underwear, which included several pairs of white, cot-ton bloomers—the open type that allowed her to pee with-out pulling her pants down—along with several chemises and numerous pairs of black silk stockings.

When she ventured to the dark, far corner of the cellar, to the right of the desk and sink, she received the biggest sur-prise of all. There hidden away was an icebox, and when she opened it, she saw it was laden with fresh fruit. And to make circumstances even better, next to it was a portable stove on top of which was a box of matches and an envelope.

Samantha had never felt so happy in all of her life. Yes, she knew that sounded ridiculous, locked away in some underground cell, but somehow it was what she felt, so much so that tears of joy ran down her face as she opened the envelope and read the letter within.

Madam. If you are reading this, then somehow our interview did not go as I expected. I know that what I am subjecting you to is unforgivable however in recompense I have left you with the best possible conveniences considering your situation. Once again, my sincerest apologies.

P.S. There are some books in the wardrobe, and a length of thin rope in the drawer of the desk that you can use as a clothesline for your washing should your stay be longer than expected. Good luck.

Samantha folded the letter and replaced it in the envelope. *What strange manner of man is this?* He had played the part of a dastardly villain only to then turn into the most benevolent of guardians. *Was it all part of his plan? His purpose to make her happy within her confines?* She would never know, but regardless of the intent, it had worked. She was extremely content, knowing that sometime soon the door above the stairs would open, and she would be freed.

Melbourne 2018

Jennifer was enraged. How dare her new companions, especially the supposed *all-knowing* dowager, place her in the same room with the man who had broken her heart and humiliated her so dreadfully only two years ago? She stormed over to H G. "What in the fuck is he doing here?"

H G's mouth opened in amazement. "That is exactly what the dowager said you would say."

"I am not surprised, given our history."

"No, you misunderstand me, Jennifer. I mean exactly, literally, what you would say."

Puzzled, Jennifer frowned. "What do mean?"

H G pulled a notebook from her jacket, flipping through the pages before stopping and briefly showing the relevant passage to her. "Here, I shall read it for you. *Upon seeing Shane Courtney, Jennifer will storm over to you and utter these words,* What in the fuck is he doing here?"

Jennifer held the notebook that remained firmly in H G's hand and looked at the words written in bold capital letters. She was astonished. *How could this be so?*

"And remember this is coming from a nineteenth century, elderly stateswoman who would no sooner use such language as she would fly to the moon," H G reiterated.

Jennifer locked eye to eye with her, seeking an explanation that could add a measure of rationality to the surrealism that was enveloping her. "Who is this woman? How can she know so much? What did she look like?"

H G's gaze wandered wistfully away from Jennifer's, her expression filled with awe. "She cut a majestic, statuesque figure as she sat there in her black dress. Her face was covered by a thick, black veil, her hands similarly covered in black lace. She spoke with the voice of a cultured woman."

She looked back at Jennifer, her attention returning to the present. "I was quite intimidated in her presence. It was as though I had stepped into a Dickens novel, such was the ambience that surrounded her."

She flourished the notebook, drawing Jennifer's attention to it. "She gave this to me. Every circumstance that has occurred up until now, such as your recent outburst of colourful language, is listed within and has come to pass with unerring accuracy. Plus, there is her knowledge of my machine and of Samantha's involvement in its development, and how that circumstance would transpire. All of this has absolutely convinced me, hence the reason for my unwavering faith in its veracity."

Jennifer remained puzzled and enraged. "So are you saying that Shane *fucking* Courtney and that murderous prick next to him are meant to be here? That they are part of this fucked-up fiasco?"

H G gaped at her. "Madam, I have spent time amongst many women, some of them the roughest of bar-room types, but never have I met one with such a tongue as yours."

Taken aback, Jennifer was suddenly self-conscious of her foul language.

H G continued. "But back to your question regarding Shane and Simon's involvement. Yes, they, like the rest of us are vital to our mission." She became animated, her face inflamed. "Indeed, the dowager has dictated how each of us shall be grouped for our campaign to ensure the success of Samantha's rescue, while also ensuring our individual destinies. About this, she is steadfast and will brook no argument. We will be arriving in London at nine, on the morning after Samantha's disappearance, so we have no time to lose."

"*Disappearance* you say." Rebecca intervened. "So she may not be kidnapped? Perhaps she is having an affair, that's what most of these cases are about, the rocks in a marriage bed."

Peter growled, clearly annoyed. "Madam, I can assure there are no such rocks in our marriage bed. We are emotionally, spiritually, and sexually entwined in all senses of the word."

H G supported Peter. "Indeed, plus the dowager has informed us of the abduction."

Rebecca nodded. "Okay then, though it pays to be thorough."

By the time the exchange had run its course, Jennifer had calmed down, although still annoyed at Shane's presence. However, the accuracy of the dowager's knowledge of her language, combined with her incredible journey in H G's machine, had convinced her that whatever path they were on could well be destined, as she had claimed.

"So how are we to be matched?" Daria enquired, clearly enthused by what was happening around her.

Jennifer looked across at her delightful friend who appeared to be having the time of her life. She was so proud of Daria and what she had achieved and was grateful to have her by her side on this most bizarre of adventures.

"I will be paired with Simon," H G said. "His skills with a knife and knowledge of things technical making him the perfect choice as my guardian."

Jennifer was shocked. *Surely, she must be joking?*

But it wasn't her voice that sounded disapproval. It was Police Inspector Rebecca Browning. "Have you lost your senses? This man is a homicidal psychopath. You are not planning to arm him?"

"Indeed I am, Inspector. Not only with the sharpest of knives but also with the knowledge of how to operate the DEMAT. He will become my back-up, my assistant, if you will."

Rebecca's mouth was agape, unable to speak, such was the level of her astonishment. Finally, her words emerged. "Miss Wells, you cannot do this. This man will kill us all in our sleep. Slice our throats without blinking an eye."

Simon glared intently at Rebecca, his cold, green eyes as animated as they could be. "No, I won't. Don't worry, I intend to slice you apart Browning, but at another time and place. I am on a journey where my destiny is about to be realised. So you, nor anyone else, need worry about me . . . for now. For now, my education from and protection of H G is my only concern."

Jennifer looked at Shane, observing his reaction to his maniacal foster brother's amazing exclamation. He was clearly flabbergasted, completely flummoxed, and surprisingly concerned, no doubt, for his brother's state of mind.

Shane's voice seemed full of care as he spoke to Simon. "Are you all right, mate? You've been acting weird all day."

Christ, don't tell me he's becoming compassionate in his old age? It was then she once again noticed just how handsome he was, memories of their loving, lustful embraces flooded through her brain. *What the fuck? What is wrong with you? He is a monster. Granted, a hellishly good-looking monster, but a monster nonetheless.*

Simon never took his gaze off H G while he replied to Shane, lending a sense of unearthliness to his words. "Ever since I learnt of my upcoming journey, I knew I was about to meet with my destiny, my true, intended fate, my rightful place in this world of ours. Your dowager is truly very wise. You and your friends need have no fear of me, Miss Wells."

It was H G's turn to be astonished, as she fumbled through the pages of her notebook until she reached the passage she sought. She then astounded everyone else in the room as she read Simon's last twelve words verbatim. *"You and your friends need have no fear of me, Miss Wells."* There was a collective gasp in the room, and she looked up to address everyone. "Surely no one can now doubt the truthfulness and accuracy of the dowager's messages. It is clear she is somehow aware of what fate befalls us all."

Everyone remained silent, Rebecca shrugging her shoulders in resignation, Daria smiling profusely, Peter Rhodes nodding his head, while Shane's mouth was still agape as he stared bewilderedly at his beloved brother, Simon, whose face was a picture of serenity.

As for Jennifer, she was thoroughly convinced and prepared to follow the dowager's instructions to the letter. Clearly, this woman was a seer, a visionary, a teller of truth.

"So that is Simon and you paired, who is to be with me?" Peter asked.

H G consulted the dowager's instructions. "It says here, and I will quote. *Peter will be grouped with Rebecca and Daria.*

Their task is to find Samantha. Rebecca's detective skills, Daria's ability to apprehend any miscreants, together with Peter's local knowledge and Victorian communicative skills making the perfect combination."

Jennifer thought that made sense until it dawned on her that the two people left unmatched were her and Shane. *This can't be so?* She turned to H G. "That leaves Shane and me together. What possible reasons could there be for this?"

H G turned to the notebook again, its stature fast beginning to take on that of a Holy text, such was the reverence it was assuming. "Allow me to quote the dowager again. *Jennifer will at this stage proclaim her displeasure and her doubt over the wisdom of her pairing with Shane, asking W*hat possible reasons could there be for this?"

Once again everyone gasped, including Jennifer. *Jesus.*

H G continued, smiling as she spoke next. "There is a side note here, next to Jennifer's quote in brackets. Let's see, it says. *Thankfully her speech this time was without the accompanying obscenities."*

Everyone laughed at this, except Jennifer, who had never felt so embarrassed. *What's with this effing dowager? It is as though she is in the bloody room with us.* She regained her composure. "So what is her reasoning? What is it Shane and I are meant to be doing together?"

"Again, I will quote the dowager. *Shane and Jennifer will be assigned the task of interviewing Samantha's friends, Phyllis and Georgina, at Doctor Rhode's London branch of his institute, which is run by* Maîtresse *Simone and her trusty assistant, Katerina. All four of these people are as sexually perverse as Shane and Jennifer, so there should be common ground."*

Shane laughed while Jennifer felt as exposed as she had ever been. *This is so fucking embarrassing.*

"Georgina and Phyllis will be there for their biannual four-hour treatment. It is very opportune." Peter stated, seemingly unperturbed by the dowager's remarks regarding the sexual nature of his clinic.

"Four-hour treatment? What treatment?" Daria asked. "On our journey over here you said your results were faultless."

Peter huffed. "Of course, they are faultless. These ongoing treatments are voluntarily taken by the ladies for the continued maintenance of their mental health, and I suspect, for their continued pleasure."

Pleasure? This sparked Jennifer's interest. "Pleasure? What do the treatments consist of?"

"The ladies are fixed to an immovable object in their institute uniforms and are vaginally massaged for four hours, experiencing several orgasms in the process."

Jennifer could not believe what she had just heard. Neither could her vagina, from which a gentle trickle had started to emerge. It was taking all her skill to conceal the physical excitement she was experiencing, and she felt the impact of Daria's intrusive stare. *Damn that girl, she knows me too well.*

She found herself looking forward to her upcoming task, instinctively glancing at Shane, who had the broadest grin on his face before startling her with his next action. He winked at her. She turned away instantly, pretending she had not seen his recognition of her predictable sensual response. *Bugger you, Courtney.* It was as though she was surrounded by people aware of her sexual proclivities, especially Shane who had used it to manipulate her when she was in love with him. *Well, that won't be happening again, matey. So keep your bloody winks to yourself.*

Rebecca's intervention was a godsend for Jennifer. The last thing she wanted was for anyone else to recognise she was being turned on by the conversation.

"I fail to see how bringing a woman to a climax under such shameful circumstances, could in any way be considered a treatment," Rebecca protested.

Rebecca's feminist feathers had obviously been ruffled, Jennifer well aware of her hatred of chauvinistic, controlling men. Her twenty-first century, lesbian views further influenced by her hatred of all forms of male dominance and the sexism she had been fighting all her working life within the chauvinistically male police force.

Consequently, Jennifer was looking forward to observing their exchange, especially considering their respective values were one hundred and twenty years apart, a clash of cultures if ever there was one.

"Maybe in your world of modernity and sexual liberation, madam, but these women are socially, morally, and sexually repressed. Are you aware that in my society it is considered physically impossible for a woman to orgasm? Indeed, if they happen to experience any such excitement they are deemed by the male-dominated medical profession to have experienced a paroxysm," Peter replied, somewhat arrogantly, though perhaps it could be better described as authoritatively. He was, supposedly, an expert in his field of Victorian women's sexuality, Jennifer suspecting he knew a great deal more about the subject than anyone else in the room.

Rebecca appeared to be absolutely bewildered while simultaneously enraged, apparently unable, however, to formulate a response.

Peter paused long enough to note Rebecca's hesitancy. "I have had over two hundred women at my institute, none of whom had experienced, nor thought possible that they could so experience an orgasm. All of whom were suffering from various maladies, ranging from deep anxiety, depression, ennui—chronic boredom—and self-harm when they came to me after having exhausted all previous avenues available to them. And all of them cured upon discovering their libidos, found via the wondrous miracle of nature's orgasm. Their lives liberated beyond measure."

His voice carried the enthusiasm and passion he clearly held about his subject matter. "Having been informed of your enlightened society by Miss Wells, I can understand your bewildered rage, madam. But you must remember that society had laden these women with impossible behavioural codes. Codes that were applied, not out of some sadistic patriarchy as you may have imagined. But designed to protect the assets of these extremely affluent gentlewomen, whose fortunes by law are immediately bequeathed to their husbands upon the completion of their nuptials. Consequently, their society's strict moral and behavioural code was deemed necessary to protect them. But in so doing, it led to a sexual repression the likes of which human society has never seen before or most likely will ever see again.

"It should also be noted that this repression, which caused an epidemic of so-called hysteria—a generic diagnosis covering all female maladies—occurred only within London society. This same hysteria was unknown amongst the working class, whose corsetry and morality were much more relaxed due to their need to be able to move freely and their lack of wealth.

"So be careful not to rush to judgement, madam, about our society, or my methods. The restraint of my patients had a duality, initially to shock them out of their entrenched repression—which they sorely needed—while relieving them of any guilt as they discovered their sexuality. Employing your own liberated experiences as a template, Miss Browning, will cause you to err on the side of ignorance, something an intelligent, fair-minded woman like yourself would surely despise, above all else."

Jennifer looked back at Rebecca, wondering what her response to such an educated and detailed argument would be and was surprised by what she saw. Clearly, Rebecca was moved by Peter's passionate oration. A single tear tumbled down one of her cheeks as she gazed at him with great compassion.

"I feel so sorry for the women in your society. I had no idea they were so suppressed. Indeed, that your whole society was so inhibited. I apologise for judging you, Dr Rhodes, clearly you are a trailblazer, a visionary, years ahead of your time. How did it come to be that you alone amongst your community are so enlightened?"

"I studied many disciplines — not just what they taught me at school — one of which was Darwin's evolutionary theory, which proves beyond doubt the natural equality of all humankind, be it by gender or by race. I then spent several years on the Continent, studying psychoanalysis under Freud, their liberal society so different from the buttoned-up values of London. After which, I spent three months at a famous French bordello, where I learnt a great deal about feminine sexuality, striking up a friendship with the resident *maîtresse*, Simone Blanchet, who now runs my London branch along with her lifetime companion, Katerina Dawson, a former patient of mine."

Intrigued, Rebecca asked, "When you say *lifetime companion*, do you mean what I think you mean?"

"If your inference is of a sapphic or lesbian relationship, then your assumption is correct. Although all their friends, including my darling wife Samantha, who is also a former patient of mine, remain completely unaware of the true nature of their alliance, such is their blissful ignorance. For example, all references to any such sapphic relationships were deleted from legislation criminalising homosexuality, simply because Queen Victoria deemed it to be, and I quote, *physically impossible.*"

He paused, glancing at everyone around the room. "Such is the level of ignorance that prevails. Consequently, all of you shall be sworn to secrecy with regards to the true nature of Simone and Katerina's relationship."

"Such innocence. It is both breathtaking and heartbreaking," Rebecca said, her voice both saddened and astonished.

"You need not worry about those two, Miss Browning. Simone is a Continental with a level of sexual intelligence that would be unrivalled in London, and indeed, even in your times. Plus, I am of the understanding that Katerina is a fast learner, if you get my drift."

Rebecca smiled broadly at Peter. "I look forward to meeting them both."

H G intervened. "As you shall, once we have completed our task and rescued Samantha, Peter's darling wife and my dearest friend. So is everyone happy with our arrangements?"

Jennifer was far from happy, but she was sure that this time around she could handle Shane, now she was aware of his duplicitous soul.

They all expressed their willingness to proceed.

London, 1898

George Best was a scoundrel, a thug for hire, so he was grateful for the opportunity to abduct the gentlewoman. However, since returning to his humble abode in White-chapel, he realised he had missed a golden opportunity. That woman, whoever she was, was obviously wealthy and her family would pay a fortune to get her back. Yet he had been instructed to leave her where she was. The gentleman who had hired him had cloaked his face when they had met in an alley at night, passing him the five guineas—a great deal of money to George—promising him many more well-paid assignments if he performed his duties satisfactorily.

At first, George had been happy with their arrangement, carrying out his task to perfection. He had stocked the room

as requested and looked forward to becoming a regular em-
ployee of the mysterious gentleman. But as he sat there in
his squalor, he realised he had a chance to make a killing.
The gentleman had no idea who George was, or where he
lived. It was true, he knew what George looked like, but
they had met on the other side of the city. Their meeting had
been arranged by a solicitor who used George's services
regularly, but who also had no idea of his name or address.
George had been introduced by an acquaintance who had
since been murdered — a frequent occurrence for people who
plied his trade.

He still had the keys to the empty warehouse and the cellar below, and to her chains. So he decided he would return
that evening, re-abducting her and bringing her to his home,
the location of which was a secret to all concerned. There-
upon, he would discover her identity and demand a ransom
from her family, escaping scot-free without killing anybody,
provided he kept his face hidden from her throughout. It
was the perfect plan, and it would set him up for life.

Chapter Five

London 1898

H G set the coordinates on the DEMAT, looking forward to what was about to ensue. She had been given explicit instructions of how she should proceed in a typed memorandum from the dowager. Indeed, her grouping of the various participants had come from them. But what she was about to do was bordering on the insane. However, such had been the accuracy of the dowager's predictions up to this point, she had long since decided that she must follow them to the letter.

There was something else that had been nagging away at her, and it concerned Shane and Daria. Something about their faces was familiar. It was not as though she recognised them—she never forgot a face—but there was something about them that intrigued her.

However, she was far too enlivened and involved with the management of her upcoming adventure to pay it much heed. The future survival of her precious time machine depended on it.

Samantha could not believe her luck. She had only been in her prison for a few hours, four or five at the most, yet the door was being opened. *My friends, they are so very clever.*

But it was not her friends that opened the door, rather a large, raw-boned ruffian, most likely the man who had abducted her in the first place. Samantha was alarmed, indeed frightened by this event, as her gentleman abductor had made no such mention of any such an occurrence. Her intruder's face was covered by a balaclava, leaving only his blue eyes and mouth visible.

"Change of plans, my lovely." He knelt down and unlocked her shackle. "You're coming with me."

He picked up the rope and roughly turned her around. Samantha was still wearing her bonnet and gloves, so quickly had everything happened, as he proceeded to bind her as before, her arms tied together behind and trussed firmly to her corseted body. He then collected the rag and bandage off the floor and once again silenced her.

Samantha was terrified. This was no gentleman who was capturing her. *God knows what plans he has for me.*

It was as though he was reading her mind. "And don't you be worryin' your pretty self about your modesty. I have no such plans for you, milady. Money is what I am after from you, and as such, I mean to treat you as a precious commodity. Now, come with me."

He tied a cloak that covered her head and torso around her, concealing her confinement from any prying eyes. Though such was the privacy of the lane above, this precaution proved needless.

"In here, madam."

Samantha was heartened by the continued respect of the terms he used to address her.

Perhaps he will be true to his word regarding my virtue. She could only hope this would prove to be so.

He lowered the tray of his covered wooden cart, lifting Samantha effortlessly into it before laying her down and affixing her wrists to her ankles. Jumping down he shut the tray, his dirty teeth smiling at her beneath his balaclava as he spoke. "Now be a good lass and stay as quiet as a mouse. If you do as you are told then not a hair on your head will be harmed, this I promise you."

He walked around and climbed onto the front seat, his covered face smiling at her over his shoulder before turning his attention to his horse, clicking it into action.

Samantha was beside herself with fear, imagining her lifeless body with its throat cut being fished from the Thames, an event she would be powerless to prevent. Moisture welled in her eyes. *Dear Lord, help me through this ordeal.*

Shane was out of his prison irons and wearing a three-piece suit with a bowler hat and sharing a carriage with Jennifer on their way to the inner London branch of Doctor Peter Rhodes's establishment, The Institute of Female Behaviour. The tension in the air between them was palpable. *Which is understandable, given our history.*

He stared at Jennifer as she sat opposite, looking out the window in a complete state of indifference. *Christ, I'd forgotten how stunning she is.* Especially as she was now attired, buttoned-up and corseted in her tailored finery, a circumstance Shane knew she would be, um, *enjoying.*

But he also knew that she knew *he* would be aware of her present euphoria, so he would have to tread warily with his words. "You look particularly lovely today, Jen. The cut of your suit exquisite."

Jennifer continued to gaze out the window, saying nothing, the expression on her face steadfastly grim.

He continued. "You know I loved you, I still do."

This she reacted to, turning her blue eyes to meet his, the coldness within sending a shiver up his spine. "*Love me?* Love me you say? I feel sorry for you, Shane Courtney, and for your twisted, controlling mind. A mind incapable of even beginning to understand the meaning of such a word."

Jesus, she despises me. Shane was taken aback by the bitterness of her vitriol, the pure hatred in her eyes burning into his soul. He was shocked. Not by her loathing, which was both deserved and expected, but by his own reaction. For the first time in his deceitful, manipulating, uninvolved life, he was hurt, his inner-being affected by another.

Upon hearing Jen's words, a deep misery had invaded his mind, his soul, and his body, completely overwhelming him. *What is happening to me?* He started to panic. *This pain is unbearable.* But try as he may, he could not rid himself of it and he found his clever, articulate mind incapable of answering her, his voice rendered mute by the terrible ache within. And then, to his complete and utter surprise, he found himself crying. Not a gentle whimpering, but a heartfelt, uncontrollable sobbing. It was as if all his repressed emotions had suddenly found an outlet, and try as he may, he could not stop their outburst.

He felt himself a fool, a weakling, exposing himself like this in front of Jennifer. But all he could do was bury his head in his hands until his emotional outburst subsided, which, after what seemed like forever, it did. He took his handkerchief from his pocket, wiping his eyes and sitting up straight, putting on a brave face in front of her. He ventured a fleeting glance into her eyes, the bravest thing he had ever done in his life, their deep blue essence causing him to once again cry uncontrollably.

Jesus, what is happening to me? His heart was aching, his soul torn apart as he sat there continuing in his anguish. Once more, it seemed forever until he stopped, this time not daring to face the reason for his pain. He had known before that day that he still loved Jennifer, thinking about her, dreaming about her every night in prison, looking forward to the day when, once again, he would make her his own. But such dreams were shown to be waves of pure folly when crashed against the rocks of her cruel detachment. He hated this feeling of torment and its accompanying vulnerability. *So this is what it means to be truly in love? Well fuck it, I despise it.*

But at the same time, Shane found himself bizarrely enraptured by his pain. What he really should have said was, *So this is what it means to be alive?* For clearly that was what he was experiencing. His emotional being, hidden away for so long to protect himself from being hurt, suddenly exposed for the world to see. And although he hated it, at the same time he cherished it. It was like the shock of a dive into icy water, at once both chilling and thrilling, the emotional and the physical coming together as one, in a blast of revelation. For the first time in his life, he felt truly alive, grief-stricken, sorrowful, mournful even, but strikingly, shockingly alive. And upon this realisation, a wave of contentment enveloped him.

He sat up and wiped his eyes, this time his smile at his beloved no longer filling him with despair. "Sorry about that," he said, trying to introduce a semblance of normality to their situation.

Strangely though, he found himself no longer embarrassed by his emotive behaviour. If he was to act like a simpleton in her presence for the rest of his days, then so be it. Never had he felt so indifferent about his own demeanour, his appearance, his mask. His emotional camouflage had been removed, but he no longer felt like a fraud without its disguise. His transformation was true, complete. He had become human — flawed, vulnerable, trusting and dreadfully afraid of the outcome, but so very glad to be alive.

Jennifer could not believe what she had just witnessed. Shane, crying like a baby in front of her, crumpled up and experiencing some sort of breakdown. But she was having none of it. She had been fooled by him before on the greatest of levels, completely giving herself, believing she had finally found the man she could share her life, her soul, with. As she watched him sobbing relentlessly before her, she wondered why he couldn't have done that when they were together. Expose his inner child, rather than always presenting himself as the perfect being, forever in control of himself and his situation, and of *her*. And it was this remembrance of his manipulation of her mind, her body, her freedom, her very existence that sent a chill across her unforgiving heart. *Never again will I believe you, Shane Courtney, never again.*

George Best carried his prisoner over his shoulder from the back yard where his stable was, far from the sight of any onlookers. As soon as he sat her on his bed, he started unwrapping her face, taking the rag from inside her mouth when he was finished. He was keen to talk to her, find out who she was so he could put his ransom plan in place.

He sat down on his wooden chair in front of the bed, facing his refined captive, his face still hidden behind the balaclava. "What is your name, madam?"

She appeared overwhelmed, beaten. "Mrs Samantha Rhodes. Please, sir, would you loosen my bonds, I am of no threat to you."

George was surprised by this. He was so focused on his task he had taken no notice of her physical condition. "Turn around."

She turned as directed, facing away from him as he sat on the bed next to her, quickly untying her from his skilful knots.

"Thank you so much." She rubbed her wrists and arms, clearly relieved to be free. They were now sitting side by side on the bed, their faces turned to each other. "You are very kind. May I ask what it is that you plan to do with me?"

"I'm going to ransom you. You will tell me who to contact and then I shall give them a drop-off point and collect the money. Then I will take you to the city in the dead of the night and leave you there."

She stared at him through fearful, moisture-filled eyes. "Truly? You are not planning to kill me?"

George was shocked by her words. Although he was a violent man, he had never used that violence against a woman. "Never would I do such a thing. Why do you think I am keeping my face hidden from you?"

She leant across and embraced him, her beautiful face resting against his chest as she let her emotions flow, sobbing quietly. This was the first time in his life he had come into contact with such a refined woman, a lady of society, and he felt overawed, beneath her.

Unsure of what to do, he tapped her on the back of her elegant jacket. "There, there, madam, you are safe with me. I wouldn't dare think of harming a female, especially one of your class." He broke from their embrace and held her upper arms glaring at her. "But I shall bind you again at some stage. Perhaps not as tightly, but I must do it so that I can sleep or leave the premises."

His threat seemed not to disturb her. She smiled at him as she replied, "I understand. You are a kind man, not at all as brutish as you look."

She seemed to realise what she had said as soon as the words came out, covering her mouth with her hand, but George was not at all offended. They stared at each other as her words sunk in, then both burst into laughter. Their mirth eased the tension in the air, and Mrs Rhodes put her hands in her lap and smiled.

"Would you like a cup of tea? Perhaps something to eat?" George had also relaxed with the ice being broken, standing up and starting his fire, over which a pot would soon be brewing and a billy boiling.

Her surprised expression had George wondering if he had overstepped the mark, forgotten his place. Even though she was his captive, such was the power of the class system in England that a person of George's upbringing knew where he stood on the ladder, and it was many, many rungs removed from a lady of Mrs Samantha Rhodes's stature.

She smiled. "Why thank you. I hadn't thought of my stomach for some while, which was why I hesitated. But now I know you are not going to cut my throat, I find myself quite at ease, and indeed famished. What have you got there?"

George was pleased, even excited by Mrs Rhodes's response. He rarely entertained, and here he was hosting a proper lady. "It is only a stew, Mrs Rhodes, but it is made from good vegetables, fresh from the market and some lamb."

Once again, she smiled. "Sounds delicious."

Jennifer stood with Shane at the doorstep of the Victorian terrace, the London branch of Dr Peter Rhodes's Institute of Female Behaviour. There was no plaque or anything that signified it was a place of business. To all outward appearances, it was just another family residence.

A young maid opened the door. Jennifer immediately announcing herself and Shane. "Jennifer Best and Shane Courtney to see *Maîtresse* Simone and Miss Katerina."

The maid smiled, ushering them into the lobby. "Yes, you are expected. Please wait here while I get the *maîtresse*."

Jennifer looked around at the opulent fittings and furniture. *Business must be booming.*

Into the room bounced a magnificent woman, voluptuous in both manner and bearing. She smiled warmly as she approached them, addressing them with the broadest of French accents. "Miss Best, Mr Courtney, how wonderful to meet you. I am Simone Blanchet, the resident *maîtresse*. H G and Pierre speak highly of you both."

Jennifer glanced at Shane. *I doubt that.* Simone held Jennifer by the shoulders and enthusiastically kissed her on both cheeks before holding out her gloved hand out for Shane to kiss, which he did as if he had been greeting women this way for all his life. *There he goes, the perfect chameleon.*

Simone wore a superbly tailored, royal blue, double-breasted suit with an IFB monogram on the breast pocket — Jennifer imagined the initials stood for Institute of Female Behaviour — together with a white collar and a black and white striped tie. She looked spectacular.

A shorter, extremely slender woman with high cheekbones and captivating light green eyes entered the lobby. She was dressed similarly, except her IFB crested uniform was of emerald green.

She spoke with an upper-class English accent. "Good morning, I am Katerina Dawson."

So this was Simone's *lifetime companion* as mention by Peter. She looked full of life and love, smiling happily at them as she, too, kissed Jennifer's cheeks and held her gloved hand out for Shane to caress with his lips.

Clearly, Simone was a woman in complete control, not in the slightest way hesitant as she addressed them. "Come into the parlour, Josephine is getting us some tea. We will have a chat about this nasty business. Poor Samantha, let's hope she is safe."

Jennifer followed the rest of them into the room, Simone and Katerina taking what she assumed to be their normal chairs. She and Shane sat opposite them, an ornate coffee table between them.

"So what is it that Peter and H G want you to find from

us?" Katerina asked.

Even though she was extremely slight in structure, Katerina had an undeniable presence, her angular features and piercing, green eyes commanding immediate attention. They were quite the couple, and had Jennifer wondering about the spectacle that they would present when making love to each other. She smiled warmly at Katerina as the maid brought the tea in on a tray.

"Leave the tray, Josephine, I will pour," Simone demanded.

As Josephine left the room and Simone poured the tea, Jennifer turned her attention back to Katerina's question. "They asked us to enquire about the last time you all saw Samantha. I understand the ladies Georgina and Phyllis are also in residence today?"

Simone smiled, a twinkle in her eye. "They are otherwise engaged for the next hour or two. But Katerina will bring them to you once they have finished their treatments."

Jennifer felt the warmth between her legs return at the mention of their four-hour treatments, glancing across at Shane in expectation of a knowing, smart-arse smirk or whatever. But he surprised her, looking directly at Simone as if he was in ignorance of her likely response. *Shit, that's a first.*

She took the cup of black tea from Simone, drinking it neat. "Peter described these treatments. They sound very interesting." She shifted on her seat, thinking about the bound ladies being sexually vibrated, having experienced similar treatment at Shane's sect. *Lucky bitches.*

"Would you like me to show you around?" Katerina asked.

Jennifer couldn't believe her luck. She wanted to say *Would I what . . .* but she toned down her response. "That would be lovely."

Katerina turned to Shane. "What about you, Mr Courtney,

would you be interested?"

Once more Jennifer expected a sardonic response from Shane, but once again he surprised her.

"No thank you, Katerina, you and Jennifer go and enjoy yourselves. Perhaps, Simone, I could talk to you, I understand Peter met you in Paris?"

"Oh, the stories I could tell you, Mr Courtney."

"Please, call me Shane. Jennifer and I would prefer if we all spoke on first name terms, wouldn't you agree, Jen?"

Pouring on the charm. There is no one better at it. "Of course." She took a sip from her cup, then followed Katerina out of the room, leaving Simone to no doubt be enchanted by her charming companion. *I wonder what his angle is, singling Simone out like that.* Shane was like a beast of prey, separating an innocent quarry from the pack to be slaughtered. She sensed, though, that Simone would give as good as she got, so Shane may be in for a bit of a shock.

H G sat at the controls of the DEMAT alongside Simon, who was now wearing a three-piece suit. "I am about to show you how to operate the DEMAT, Simon, but first I thought I should give a history lesson. As with all histories, it gives the listener a proper perspective, a greater understanding of what stands before you today."

Simon seemed entranced by the console, examining the instrument panel and the various buttons.

"Simon, are you listening?"

He turned, looking her straight in the eye, and for the first time, she saw the measure of menace within his cat-like green eyes, the blackness of his soul mirrored by their murderous intent. An involuntary shiver travelling up her spine as she looked at her deadly companion. *Dearest dowager, I hope you know what you are doing.*

But as quickly as his menace had appeared, it was replaced by a cold, impassionate gaze accompanied by a gentle, friendly smile that, to H G, was as every bit threatening as his barbarous stare.

"I am all ears, Miss Wells. Please, continue."

If it was her deadly companion's intent to put her on edge, then he was extremely successful. "As I was saying" — she cleared her throat, doing her best to sound commanding — "this short history will serve to give you a true perspective of the updated machine." She peered into the green monsters that stared back at her, one of the bravest things she had ever done. "What I am about to tell you is something I have never told anyone before, not even Samantha, indeed, *especially* not Samantha. So I trust we can keep it between ourselves?"

Simon smiled, his perfect white teeth prominent as he spoke. "You can trust me with your life, Miss Wells, as I am sure you are already well aware."

Indeed, she did know what he meant, well aware that he could easily take one of the knives sheathed beneath his jacket and, without blinking an eye, cut her throat. It was as though, once armed, he had become the homicidal monster he truly was. H G swallowed nervously, the dowager had been adamant that it was necessary, as was the act of arming him if everything was to happen as it should. "The original machine that I built with Samantha's mathematical assistance was extremely primitive."

Simon suddenly stopped his inspection of the console and stood. His attention was fully on her, continuing his cold stare. "Go on."

"It was a machine for two that used the power of electricity, which allowed Samantha and I to travel to the year twenty-seventy-eight so we could find a new power source and update our knowledge. Using the science that was now available to us, the very clever Samantha showed me how to redesign our machine and how we could use nuclear energy as our source, which we did, eventually returning in the DEMAT that we stand in today."

Simon's gaze fixed firmly on H G, though thankfully no longer in a murderous way. "So nuclear energy was powerful enough?"

"Oh yes." H G was becoming relaxed. "Nuclear energy is very powerful. Would you like me to explain?"

"Go ahead." Simon was clearly engaged.

"As you know, Einstein came up with his famous formula, E=MC2, which is a way of expressing nuclear energy, which has taken on an esoteric dimension when in actual fact it is quite simple. If you remember in school, we were all taught that the energy of an object is equal to its mass times its velocity, E=MV2. The C in the new formula represents the speed of light, the maximum speed that any object can travel through space. So what he has done is replace the V, the arbitrary velocity in the old formula, with C. All the new formula E=MC2 is saying, is that energy equals mass times the maximum speed possible. As light's speed is three-hundred-thousand kilometres a second, an astronomical figure, this produces unbelievable amounts of energy." H G picked up a paper clip. "For example, the maximum energy of this clip could power a twenty-first-century family car for a hundred years."

Even Simon seemed impressed by her knowledge.

H G continued. "So the uranium within the DEMAT will last us for centuries. Samantha is completely unaware of her time travel and the advanced, relativistic knowledge she learnt while in the future. A knowledge that is destined to be acquired over many decades, not in the year eighteen-ninety-eight. As you know, nuclear power can be a tremendously destructive force that, if discovered earlier than it was and placed into the hands of a monster like Hitler, may well have caused Armageddon. Thus, Samantha had to be relieved of this future knowledge, the Victorian era not ready for it."

"But what about you, you are aware?"

"So are you, but what could you do about it?"

"Nothing, I don't have the skills."

"Exactly. And neither do I. Only someone with Samantha's mathematical genius could make use of the knowledge, as displayed by the DEMAT. Samantha and I sat down and agreed that she should not carry that knowledge back to the nineteenth century."

"How did you do that?"

"Good question, and this is the component of the DEMAT's operation that is of your concern. As I explained to your colleagues, one of the basic tenets of time travel is that no one can be in the same place at the same time as their previous incarnation. If you travel back in time and appear while in the presence of your former self, your second incarnation will instantly dematerialise, or disappear if you prefer."

Simon's eyes opened wide. "Amazing. So this is what you did to Samantha, dematerialised her second self by bringing her back to a moment in time before you left."

"Precisely."

Simon's gaze turned away, clearly deep in thought. "So Samantha would have no knowledge of the DEMAT? Very clever," he mumbled as if to himself. His attention snapped back, addressing her directly. "So as far as she is concerned, she designed the first machine but has no idea of its travels, in either of its forms."

"Exactly. I am glad you understand. But all that is about to change as Peter is already aware, so I shall bring her up to speed once she is rescued."

Simon looked away again, smirking. "So knowing that I

must never return to a moment before I leave is very important, if I want to retain my memory of the journey."

"The trick is to land at a place and a time where you are not physically present."

"But if that is where you currently exist, aren't you ever-present?"

"Another great question."

Simon looked chuffed.

"The secret lies in the definition of one being *physically present*. Samantha estimated that area to be approximately five metres when the life force of an object would be felt by the other. And as ever, her calculated prediction proved to be correct. This was approximately the distance where the second Samantha dematerialised."

"So if I returned to twenty-eighteen England, I could co-exist with the Simon in an Australian jail?"

"Technically you could, but of course that particular Simon is about to leave in a time machine, so the point is moot."

"Thank you for all that. Now, more importantly, show me how to work this thing."

"Certainly."

H G was pleased. Simon was now completely aware of the power of the DEMAT and how to avoid being dematerialised, exactly as the dowager had wished. Now all he had to do, like the rest of the protagonists—including her—was to follow his natural desires, thus fulfilling his predestined path.

CHAPTER SIX

London 1898

Samantha had slept in reasonable comfort the night before. Having established a relationship with her captor, they found themselves conversing on all kinds of matters. Although uneducated, he was an intelligent and caring man, using only the shackle, chain, and padlocks he had taken from the cellar to fasten her ankle to the bed. He had not gagged her, taking her at her word that she would remain silent. Besides he would sleep on the floor in front of the door, promising her that if he heard her scream, he would immediately bind and gag her as cruelly as before.

As she awoke, she saw her captor was still asleep. No doubt the contents of the empty bottle of wine by his side the reason for his extended slumber. She watched him snoring loudly, lost from the world, and for a brief moment, she thought of venturing over and stealing the keys and absconding. But she decided it was too risky. Plus, she did not want to destroy the trust she had built between them, a trust that was vital to the brilliant idea that had hatched within her mind overnight. It was a daring, outrageous plan, but one Samantha was certain she could pull off.

He started to stir then woke up, looking around before focusing on Samantha as if he had forgotten all about her. He no longer wore his balaclava, discarded as their friendship grew throughout the evening. He sat up and smiled. "Good morning, Mrs Rhodes. I see you were as good as your word, thank you for that." He crossed the room and unshackled her ankle. "I suppose you have a need for the toilet, I know I have."

"Please, you go first. I am sure my need is less pressing."

"Thank you." He walked across to the toilet bowl and urinated in front of Samantha, who averted her gaze, her Victorian modesty coming to the fore. She heard him finish, then watched as he went to the fireplace and started a new fire with his back to her. "Your turn now. I shall keep my eyes to the front. Would eggs and a cup of tea do you for breakfast?"

"That would be lovely." Samantha went across to the toilet and sat down, keeping a vigilant eye on her captor as she relieved herself, lest he should renege on his word.

Sitting back down on the bed she began the conversation she hoped would lead to her freedom with the minimum of fuss. "I was thinking about your ransom plan overnight, and I believe it is doomed for failure."

He stopped stoking the fire and turned around to face her, maintaining his squatting position.

"Do you now?"

"I do, for instance, the drop-off of the ransom money. They will be watching you and will follow you back here."

"I'm not coming back here. I will leave you here bound and gagged informing them when I give my original ransom demand that you are buried underground and that your very survival depends on my safe departure. Your true location will be given to them some two hours later by a prearranged messenger."

"They will still follow you, wait until I am found, then arrest you. But let's not concern ourselves with that. How much is your demand?"

"One thousand guineas. I intend to go to the Americas where such a sum would enable me to buy a home and establish a business. Perhaps even start a family, a likely prospect I am told in such a classless society."

"I have an even better proposition. One that would deliver you two thousand guineas and a hero's welcome."

His eyebrows raised. "What manner of nonsense is this? Tis not possible, Mrs Rhodes."

"Oh, but it is, especially if you were my rescuer, not my abductor."

His expression turned from one of doubt to one of measured thought. "Go on."

"My proposition is this. You and I will go to a particular residence around one in the afternoon where most everybody I know will be gathered due to a particular arrangement. Once there I will introduce you as my rescuer and make contact with my husband, Doctor Peter Rhodes, who will immediately join us. Then, upon his arrival, I will propose that you be rewarded the amount of two thousand guineas, an amount which my husband and I will happily pay. He may well reward you more for I am the love of his life, as he is mine."

He looked at her with a mixture of disbelief and bewilderment. "How can I be sure you will not betray me?"

She hesitated before continuing. "May I enquire of your name?" *This will make us even more familiar.*

He considered her request. "I suppose it don't matter, either way. Either you'll be safely tied up here and I will have decamped, or I will be like Daniel in the lion's den where my name will be announced to all and sundry. It is Best, George Best."

"The reason I shall not betray you, Mr Best, is pure and simple. Firstly, I am in fact eternally grateful to you for taking me from that hole. Who knows, I may have been there for weeks, even months. Plus, as a person of public standing, as indeed is my husband, the last thing he or I would want is any such notoriety. Two thousand guineas is a small price to pay to avoid such a scandal."

He turned back to his fire, quietly stoking it for a moment's pause. "I shall need to think about it. It does sound attractive, and two thousand guineas would set me up handsomely in the new world."

"We have plenty of time." She looked at her fob watch. "It is nine o'clock. We have four hours up our sleeve."

"We have four hours up our sleeve if I accept your proposition, whereas if I proceed with my plan, I shall have to make contact this hour."

She watched in trepidation as he stood and placed the billy, then the frypan, above the flame, breaking four eggs into it. "I shall feed us first, then I shall decide what to do."

Jennifer followed Katerina as she showed her around the house. It was a delightful terrace home, much like her own in St Kilda. As she talked to Katerina, she sensed she was with a woman far more liberated in her views than many people from the twenty-first century. Here was a lady at peace with herself, content with her lot as the lifetime companion of her lover.

After showing Jennifer the upstairs, kitchen, and the beautiful back garden, they walked back into the house. Katerina suddenly became very serious. "What I am about to show you may shock you, Jennifer."

"I doubt that."

"Within this next chamber there are four treatment rooms, rooms where former patients of Mr Rhodes's institute partake in various ongoing maintenance exercises for their mental and sexual wellbeing."

"Yes, Peter informed us of them on our journey here."

Katerina looked surprised. "Surely you mean after your

journey from the Antipodes, not during it?"

Jennifer silently admonished herself. *I keep forgetting my situation.* She chuckled. "Of course, Doctor Rhodes is hardly likely to have gone to and from Australia in a few hours?"

"Precisely. But I am more surprised that Peter told you of his methods, something about which he is normally very circumspect. I suspect it is to do with the extraordinary circumstances we find ourselves in."

"Probably." Jennifer was being as brief as possible, very eager to see the contents and arrangements of the four rooms.

Katerina unlocked the large door that led into a dimly lit passageway that had two doors on each side. "The rooms are soundproof so we can speak normally. Georgina and Phyllis are enclosed in the front chambers."

Enclosed? Chambers? She felt her vagina stirring at the thought of being fastened inside such a confined space attached to a vaginal massager, as they were called in this amazing era.

Katerina unlocked the first door on her left, opening it back toward the passage. Jennifer was enthralled, her mind and body aflame as she ventured ever so carefully inside. Immediately inside the small room hung a red curtain that draped gently to the floor, about two feet away from the door. Pulling it back, Katerina revealed a small room, about three metres by two, its length running parallel to the door. Its walls were covered with red velvet and in its middle stood a small, circular, red velvet post that rose from a lushly carpeted floor, the post facing a triple-pane mirror.

Fuck me. This is so sensual, so beautiful.

"This is the Kneeling Room, where patients can partake of a silent, peaceful, sexual four-hour vaginal massage experience, viewing themselves in their institute uniform as they kneel, gagged and bound strictly to the post. As you can imagine it is very sensual."

Jennifer's vagina was dripping as she took in the carnal ambience of the room. The sexuality of the situation overwhelmed her, so much so that she very nearly fell to her knees, steadying herself against the wall.

Katerina noticed her distress, clearly mistaking it as a violation of her modesty. "Are you all right, Jennifer? I did warn you."

She gently took hold of Jennifer's elbow, this lightest of touches causing a ripple of sensuality that travelled throughout her body. Never had she felt so tactile, so sensually aware.

Jennifer was about to reply that she was fine, but the magnetism of the room was drawing her into its adorable clutches. "Warn me? You did not warn me sufficiently, Katerina. This room is magnificent, electrifying. No, I am not fine. I'm not sure how you would describe it here in Victorian London, but I am so turned on."

"Turned on? I have never heard such an expression." She held Jennifer's face in one hand, squeezing her cheeks firmly, looking her squarely in the eye. "But judging by the dilation of your pupils I can hazard a guess you are referring to your nether regions."

What she did next both shocked and delighted and indeed intoxicated Jennifer. Keeping Jennifer's cheeks within her hand and her eyes fixed upon hers, she put her glove in her teeth and took it off. She then pulled up Jennifer's elegant skirt and began to digitally explore her, finally resting her hand within her extremely welcoming, moist pussy. Jennifer screamed, her mind and body on fire.

Katerina pressed her hand over her mouth and threw her against the wall, resting her own body against Jennifer's as she continued to dominate her with both her eyes and her finger. "So you are excited, madam? You wish to play?"

Jennifer slowly nodded her head in the affirmative, her

eyes not for one second leaving the dominant gaze of her companion.

Katerina stopped, taking one hand away from Jennifer's mouth, the other from within her body. She stepped back and gently stroked Jennifer's tailored finery back into place. *Fuck, how does she know me so well?* Jennifer was dripping, but without any embarrassment, the sensual ambience of the place, together with the overt sexuality of her companion leaving no room for any such modesty.

She watched as Katerina opened a wardrobe behind her, extracting several coils of silky-smooth hemp rope and throwing them onto the floor behind the post. Then she placed a red satin cushion at the foot of the post nearest the mirror.

"Kneel child and place your hands behind the posts for me."

Age wise, Katerina had no right to refer to her as a *child*, but sexually she had every right. She was as putty in the mistress's hands, her every desire Jennifer's every command. *Oh, dear God, this is unbelievable.* Her heart was beating alarmingly as she knelt before the mirror, its three-pane elegance displaying the magnificence of her superbly costumed torso. Her body was aflame with desire, her vagina wildly discharging its moisture of joy. She had lost all control as she watched and felt her beautiful body being expertly bound to the post, each tug of rope taking her further from freedom and closer to the paradise of her dreams.

The symmetry of Katerina's rope work was perfection, an artist in complete control of her craft as Jennifer knelt before her, the post and her as one. She stroked Jennifer's cheek, Jennifer responding with a kiss as Katerina's finely gloved hand passed gently over her face.

"Two more pieces. My *pièce de résistance* as Simone would say. Then I shall leave you alone my lovely."

Jennifer was afire with anticipation as she awaited these final pieces. She could barely move, her body from neck to knees trussed to the post, her arms pinioned together behind it while further rope pressed her arms and body together. Her feet were drawn up behind her, her heels touching her elbows as Katerina came back and placed a thin, kid leather gag with a large round plug both over and within her delicate mouth, silencing her.

She was in heaven, her vagina dripping. *What more could her captor do?* And then she saw it, a large instrument with a huge knob that Katerina tied between the ropes entwining her body, placing it precisely at a place over her skirt at the level of her clitoris. She turned on the instrument before lightly touching Jennifer's shoulder, then drew the curtain and locked Jennifer within her soundproof cocoon, leaving her to her private ecstasy.

Jennifer was gushing, her underclothes saturated, and when she felt the incessant throbbing of the coarse instrument against her vagina she exploded, screaming wildly through her gag as she opened and closed her eyes, catching glimpses of her beautiful imagery captured in the mirror before her.

However, the other images that flashed through her brain hit her like a thunderbolt, the disturbing flashes resonating on her brain as she knelt there, unable or unwilling to dismiss them from her mind. They were of Shane, beautiful, handsome, glorious Shane. Tears were pouring from her eyes as she realised that her heart remained a prisoner to his very being, her mind as captive to her own desires as her body was to Katerina's ropes.

She bowed her head in resignation, her lust expired, admitting defeat. He would always be in her heart, her mind, her soul. Tears tumbled down her cheeks as she felt the misery of her situation. *Oh, why can't I forget you? Why do you haunt me so?*

The door crashed open and the curtain was savagely drawn. And there stood Shane.

George Best stood beside Samantha as she rang the doorbell of Simone and Katerina's home. He had agreed to Samantha's terms, deciding to put his trust in her. They had arrived earlier than Samantha had suggested, before noon, as George was anxious to get it over with. If he had been duped by this beautiful woman, then so be it. But something about her spoke truth. She seemed an open soul without a duplicitous bone in her body, so he had agreed to put his head in her velvet noose, praying that his faith would be rewarded.

The maid answered the door and upon opening it screamed with delight as she espied Samantha, hugging her fiercely. *Clearly, she is much-loved, even by the servants. Perhaps my judgement about her is correct.*

The maid stopped her embrace, admonishing herself for her lack of control. "I am so sorry, Miss Samantha, I forgot myself." She ran back into the main body of the house, screaming loudly. "*Maîtresse* Simone, Miss Katerina, it is Samantha, she is back home, safe and sound."

George watched as two women, one tall and curvy, the other slender and petite ran into the lobby followed by a red-headed, strikingly handsome man. The two women embraced Samantha wildly, smothering her with kisses.

The large one's voice was full of exuberance as she held Samantha by the shoulders, shaking her vigorously. "We thought you may be dead, taken from us forever." She hugged her warmly again, pressing her cheek against Samantha's, her eyes closed, her expressive, attractive face beaming.

George noticed the auburn man talking to the slender lady, before taking a set of keys off her and rushing down the hallway. It was then that the enthusiastic, taller lady noticed him, stepping away from Samantha and looking him up and down. "And who is this fine, strong mark of a man?"

"Simone, this is George Best. He is my rescuer." Samantha replied.

Without hesitation, Simone stepped up and embraced him, which surprised George considering the ragged state of his clothes. Clearly, she was a woman of little or no inhibition, or hesitation, her Continental accent perhaps explaining this trait. His arms were pressed against him in her vigorous embrace as she kissed him warmly on both cheeks. "How can we ever repay you for your noble deed, kind sir?"

"That has been decided upon by my good self as we travelled over here in Mister Best's wagon," Samantha replied. "George is desirous of leaving our shores to look for a better life, and I intend to sponsor him in recompense."

"As indeed shall Katerina and I. What are you suggesting?"

"I was thinking two thousand guineas."

"Excellent, we shall match it, as perhaps Phyllis and Georgina may, once they realise you were abducted."

"You didn't tell them?"

Katerina smiled mischievously. "We didn't want to spoil their treatment."

"Quite right." Samantha nodded.

George could not believe his ears. These women were throwing around fortunes, at least to a man of his means, as if they were confetti.

"Quickly, ring Peter and let him know of my safe return. Where is he?'

"He rang us earlier. He is at the auditorium where you last spoke before your disappearance, interviewing the staff. Apparently, there is also an inspector from Australia that has been summoned to assist them. Katerina will call him at once."

Samantha appeared as surprised as George was bewildered, the hectic state of affairs amongst people of so much better class overwhelming him.

"From Australia? How could she get here so quickly? Did she use Mr Wells's time machine?"

Everyone laughed enthusiastically at this suggestion, except, of course, for George who was by now absolutely flummoxed. *Time machines? What manner of madness have I walked into? Are all society people like this?*

Simone must have noticed his confusion for she smiled and took him by the arm, walking him toward what George assumed was her parlour. "Come with us, you poor man. Let's have some tea and cakes and enjoy the moment."

George felt completely out of place. He didn't belong here with such a fine manner of people. He went to move his arm, but Simone had a firm hold on it, and she was strong. George could feel her power. "I am happy to eat in the kitchen, *Maîtresse* Simone."

"Nonsense, we'll be having none of that. There is no English class system within these walls, so sit yourself down on our beautiful furniture and relax. For what you did today you shall be treated as royalty."

George did as he was told, sitting down in the finest chair he had ever sat his humble arse in. He looked across at Samantha who was also seated. She winked at him and smiled. "I told you they were generous people, Mr Best."

"Aye, that they are, Mrs Rhodes, that they are."

Graham Jenkins awoke the next day full of guilt. Leaving Samantha Rhodes chained in the cellar was unforgivable. His had planned to leave so many clues as to her whereabouts that she would be found post haste. But even so, it was damned abominable to leave a refined gentlewoman in such squalor, even with all the amenities he had left her.

He was a sophisticated gentleman himself, a scholar as well as an industrialist, his readings centred on the world of science, Samantha's world. And especially in her particular field, physics, where all sorts of advances were being made in electricity, astronomy, the atomic structure, and even more particularly, the very nature of time itself. Indeed, he had become obsessed with the concept of time travel, which is why he had resorted to such drastic measures. But by late morning his conscience had got the better of him.

Consequently, he had taken his carriage down to his vacant warehouse with a plan to toss the key to her shackle down to her. Then leave her to her own devices to find her way home.

He looked at his watch as he stood outside the building. Eleven-thirteen. She had been down there approximately seventeen hours, with at least eight hours of that, he imagined, being spent in sleep, so she should be fine. He looked around to make sure there was no one about then put on his mask before placing the key in the door.

As he opened the lock, he felt the coldest of chills and a presence behind him. He spun around in absolute dread but there was nothing, nor anyone there. *Such strangeness.* He had never experienced such an ungodly feeling as what he had felt that moment, its evilness confirming his decision to free the poor woman. *God forgive me for my cruelty.*

He opened the cellar door and looked down, preparing to throw the key to Mrs Rhodes. But she was not there. Once again, a surreal feeling enveloped his soul. *How can this be?* Panicking somewhat, Graham ran down the stairs, looking around for her, but she was gone, as was the chain and the ropes.

This made no sense at all. If her friends had found her, and he highly doubted they had at this early stage, why would they bother to take the chain and the ropes? No this was the work of an abductor, and there was only one other person alive that knew she was there. *God help her.*

He raced to his carriage, deciding to make contact with H. G. Wells, admitting his involvement in Mrs Rhodes's disappearance and his reasons for doing so. But not being a fool, he would take with him some insurance, the revealing photos, using them as a bargaining tool to keep H. G. Wells from informing the authorities. He knew that the last thing H. G. would want was for his prized machine to become public knowledge.

CHAPTER SEVEN

London 1898

H G left Simon alone with the DEMAT when the phone rang. It was Katerina, informing her that Samantha had been found alive and well and was at the institute's London branch. H G was one of the few people aware of the branch's location, informing Katerina that she would be there within the hour.

She then turned to her next problem. What to do with Simon when she was away? She knew she could not trust him, but the dowager had stressed that Simon had an important part to play. So trust him she must.

Simon was still in the DEMAT when H G returned, staring at the console intently. "I have to go, Simon, Samantha Rhodes has been found, and my presence is required."

Simon looked up at her with his cold, green eyes, smiling his smile that no matter which way he shaped it always seemed menacing to her. "That's okay. I am still learning about this console, it is very complicated. You go ahead, I'll be fine."

H G was leaving this homicidal maniac alone, armed to the teeth with a time machine at his disposal. *Learning about the console? He knows exactly how to use it.*

She smiled and left him, wishing him well with his endeavours, and praying that the dowager was right.

Shane had opened the booth in which Jen had been installed, both shocked and delighted by the spectacle he saw. The superbly attired beauty was on her knees, lashed to a post and clearly experiencing some sort of sexual climax. She looked amazed by his presence. Her eyes wide open but also full of tears. *The poor darling.*

The Shane of old would have taken advantage of the situation in some way, but since his cathartic experience, such imaginings were far from his mind. His thoughts instead centred on Jennifer and only Jennifer. This was the first test of his new being, his grown-up soul, and he was passing with flying colours—his very nature concerned with her welfare not his own. But even more importantly, he felt no need to manipulate the situation, to shape it for his benefit. He no longer had to mould anything as he was strong enough and confident enough to take on the world on his terms as the person he was, a person he was beginning to admire.

He knelt and removed the gag from Jennifer's mouth, wiping off her excess saliva with his handkerchief. "Jen, I have great news." He was about to tell her about Samantha when Jennifer astounded him.

"Kiss me, my darling, kiss me."

Kiss me? Christ, he so wanted to kiss her. His body was burning with desire for her, especially in such a vulnerable pose, but he resisted. "First, my darling"—*that came out so naturally*—"let me release you. You are in an excited state of mind and I don't wish to take advantage." *Did I really just say those words?*

She gazed at him with loving eyes as he loosened her bonds, turning her head around to see him and then watching at him in the mirror as he knelt behind her.

Shane concentrated on his task, only occasionally looking at her beautiful blue eyes in the mirror, doing his best to resist the temptation of taking her in his arms and kissing her tenderly. He knew he was taking a risk, that the moment may pass, but if that is what was to happen, then so be it. He wanted her love, more than anything in the world, but not on any induced terms. *If she wants me, then she can have me as I truly am, without embellishment.*

After a few minutes, Jennifer was free, and after Shane helped her to her feet they stood together in the enclosed space, facing each other, their lips centimetres apart.

Jennifer turned away from him, eying herself in the mirror as she straightened her clothes. Shane's heart sank. But then she turned back and put her arms on his shoulders, her hands clasped behind his neck as she smiled lovingly at him. "*Now* will you kiss me, my love?"

He felt the moisture in his eyes as he took her in his arms and kissed her with a depth of feeling and tenderness he never thought possible. *She wants me.* And she wanted him just as he was. He felt so empowered by her love, a love born of pure affection for another, free from manipulation of any kind. He became a man that day, a person vulnerable to another's feelings, a human being.

Simon turned on the machine. He knew exactly where he was going and exactly what he was about to do. His first stop, Buck's Row in Whitechapel, the scene of the Ripper's first murder, Mary Ann Nichols, on Friday the 31st August 1888. Her body had been discovered at three forty AM, so he set the time for two to be sure.

At first, he planned to witness the killings, but when H G had armed him with his knives, his plans had changed. Instead of watching the Ripper's deadly executions, Simon had decided to usurp him. Kill the women himself and leave the Ripper dumbfounded. He knew exactly how each one had been murdered so he would *copy-cat* him, but in advance of the event, not after. *What a stroke of genius.* The Ripper would be enraged, possibly kill more women as a result. He would look up the history of his crimes upon his return and see what chaos his interference had caused.

The machine started, the noise filling his ears as he set the coordinates and within seconds he was where he wanted to be. He donned the broad brim hat and cloak he had found in the DEMAT's wardrobe, then stepped into the foggy street, hiding in the shadows as he waited for his prey to arrive. His cold heart was as impassionate as ever. But just as with his first, and up until this moment, his only murder, his mind was aflame. He had arrived way too early, but Simon's detached soul was perfect for the waiting game, impatience, like love, an emotion foreign to him.

Then she appeared, a small woman, only five-feet-two in height and of medium build. He came out of the shadows, startling her but she soon recovered, smiling at him. She had brown eyes and a nice smile.

"Good sir, you frightened me so."

He smiled at her. "Nothing to be frightened of here, my lovely. Are you Mary, Mary Ann Nichols?"

She looked surprised but not alarmed. "So my reputation precedes me?"

This time Simon's smile was genuine, born out of pure joy. "Oh, indeed it does, dear lady, indeed it does." He took her arm and dragged her into the shadows.

"My, aren't we the eager one? What's your fancy, sir? A good old-fashioned cock suck, or a knee trembler against the wall? I won't lay down for you, not on these filthy streets."

"That's okay, standing is fine."

He turned her around, pushing her face against the wall. "So you're a from-the-behind man, aye? That's understand-able I'm not the prettiest—"

Her words were brutally cut short by Simon's sharp blade, as was her tender throat. Twice. He used the large knife, the one with the jagged edge. These were the wounds inflicted on her according to the records, Simon desperate to replicate precisely the Ripper's actions so as to infuriate him even further.

He knelt over her lifeless body, then pulled her skirt up before plunging the knife into her abdomen. Then, true to his idol's history, he made several more incisions across her belly, using a violent, downward action as described in the records, together with four more cuts across the right side of her torso, all the wounds about fifteen to twenty centimetres in length.

Simon could be precise at his task because he was as calm as could be, his heartbeat failing to rise throughout his exertions. The triumph of his life was not a frenzied killing but a planned, exact execution, meticulously performed in accordance with the London Police's exhaustive, detailed records.

Simon felt more satisfied than elated. He had performed well under pressure, mimicking his idol's attack, and as he walked back to the DEMAT he thought of the dismayed look on the Ripper's face as he discovered the killing that was meant to be his. *Up yours mate. You're not the only crazy bastard in town anymore.*

Simon returned the DEMAT to H G's residence, careful to return to a time after he had left so that he would not dematerialise, thus retaining the striking memories of his glorious feats. He had time travelled to the remaining four murders definitively known to be Jack the Ripper's, duplicating them religiously, his knife work becoming more skilled with each slaying. He had committed to memory his victim's names, out of respect, as they were important people in his life— Mary Ann Nichols, Annie Chapman, Elizabeth Stride, Catherine Eddowes and Mary Jane Kelly.

They all appeared to be nice enough people that he didn't particularly want to kill, but they were a means to an end.

He would have loved to have stayed to witness the startled look on the Ripper's face as he came across the corpses, but he dared not risk it. Instead, he looked forward to re-reading the historical accounts.

He immediately left the DEMAT and went to the London Library in St James's Square where a comprehensive collection of London newspapers were kept. And it was there that Simon became annoyed. Not enraged, that would require some emotion, but upset. There was no change to the historical records. There was a list of *possible* rather than probable murders linked to Jack the Ripper, but no additional slayings on any of the five nights where he had intervened. This both surprised and disappointed him. Clearly, the Ripper had not reacted to his intrusion. Simon was expecting accounts of double murders on all, or at least some, of the nights in question.

Perhaps it was too dangerous for this to happen, or perhaps he was as cold-blooded as Simon, impossible to upset. And there was, of course, another possibility. That time-travel intervention does not affect history as H G claimed. He would confront her about that when she returned from her party, or whatever it was she was participating in at the institute branch. H G had left him with the address in case he wanted to join them, but the library was more important to him than some celebration of an entitled bitch's rescue.

He walked back into H G's home just as the phone was ringing. He thought he should answer it in case it was H G. "Hello."

A strong, resonant male voice came down the line. "I wish to speak with Hope Grace Wells."

"She's not here."

"Can you tell me where she is? My name is Graham Jenkins. I am an acquaintance of her cousin, the other H. G. Wells. He suggested I ring her at this number."

"Hold on." He put the phone down and retrieved the piece of paper with the branch's address on it, then returned. "Fifteen Hill Street, Mayfair."

"Thank you for your assistance, kind sir. Can I enquire as to your name?"

"No." He hung the phone up and just as he did H G walked into the room. "You're back?"

She smiled. "Yes, I am. I wanted to see how you were faring. Who was that on the phone?"

"A Graham Jenkins. He's going to the branch to talk to you, urgently so he says."

H G shrugged. "I'll be there to greet him. You and I need to talk."

Good, there was something he wanted to talk to her about, too.

H G turned to Simon before they sat in her parlour. "Would you like something to drink?"

"Normally I would say no, but I have something big to celebrate, so why not?"

H G went across to the bar and poured two sherries, adding a powder to Simon's glass. She stirred the glass, careful to keep her actions hidden. It was time to take control of him.

She handed him the glass. "Bottoms up, old man."

"Bottoms up," Simon responded accordingly before swallowing the drink with one gulp.

H G was startled by this but also happy. *Good, he should be asleep in five or so minutes. But first I need to confirm a few facts.* "So what are we celebrating, Simon?"

Simon smiled happily, obviously the alcohol, not the substance, taking immediate effect. Pointing his finger at her, he scowled with feigned anger. "You, H G, are full of shit."

"Is that so?"

"Yes, that's so. Time travel does not affect history."

"And what are you basing that on, Simon? Your recent sojourn to Whitechapel?"

For the first time, at least that H G had witnessed, Simon showed some reaction, his impassionate eyes blinking rapidly.

"So you know about that?" His words were starting to slur. "That's good, it makes it easy."

"Makes what easy, Simon?"

"I went back to the Ripper's murders. At first, I was just going to observe the man but when you gave me those knives . . ." He smiled at her, his palms open, his eyebrows raised, his head slightly cocked. "What else was I to do? I usurped him."

"Usurped him?"

"Yes." His words were now genuinely slurred. "I killed them before he did. But then I go to the library and nothing's bloody changed, his history unaltered. Your theories are bullshit, *bullshit*." He tried to stand up to emphasise his point but he was clearly incapable.

"Did it ever occur to you Simon that you didn't usurp him?"

"What are you talking about?"

"That there was no one to usurp."

Simon glared at her, his drunken, drug-induced mind trying to make sense of what she had said.

"That *you*, in fact, are Jack the Ripper."

At first, Simon looked bewildered, but then his face changed, morphing into one of pure delight. "You clever bitch, you tricked me. You turned me into Jack the bloody Ripper."

"I turned you into nothing, Simon. You are who you are. But now at least we understand why he—you—was never found."

Simon flopped onto the couch, still smiling. Then he fell asleep.

H G lifted him up and threw him over her shoulder. He was surprisingly light, belying the gravity of his murderous existence. Returning to the DEMAT, she propped Simon up against one of the benches, before going to a locker and retrieving a set of the prison transport irons.

Within minutes Simon was fully restrained and attached to a post of a bench. He was going nowhere. Well, that was not strictly correct. Simon was going somewhere, but with H G in the DEMAT. Under instruction from the dowager, H G had previously travelled to Scotland in 1310, making contact with King Robert the Bruce, the sudden appearance of the DEMAT shocking him into a reverent state. She had promised to return within five minutes—which she was about to do—with a warrior supreme who would create havoc amongst his enemies in his wars for independence, which was not going well. H G was taking Simon to a time and place where his barbarous soul belonged, where his fighting, murderous ways would be revered by his soon-to-be contemporaries who shared many of his merciless traits.

She looked at Simon as she started the DEMAT. *Finally, you shall be where you belong.* H G knew that someone like Simon could never find true peace, but this warring environment would give him the closest thing possible, and strangely, as she watched him lying there, she wished him well.

The doorbell of the institute rang again, this time a tall, distinguished gentleman entering. He introduced himself as Graham Jenkins, and, as he spoke, his resonant voice immediately registered with one person in particular. Samantha Rhodes. *It is my gentleman kidnapper.* She looked across at

George Best who also seemed to have recognised the voice, a look of alarm spreading across his face.

Just then, H G entered the room, carrying a set of clothes on a hanger. The gentleman caller addressed her. "Are you Miss Wells? Just the person I wanted to see."

H G walked purposefully over to him, smiling as she took his arm. "As I do you, good sir, but not here." She led him to the room next door, but not before taking Samantha aside. "Bring Mr Best and follow me."

The four of them stood in the room, the waiting room for the branch's patients. H G took command. "Samantha, the two gentlemen in this room are responsible for your abduction, one of whom you are well aware, the other . . ."

Samantha glared at Graham. "I know it was Mr Jenkins, H G, I would recognise that voice anywhere."

Graham started to respond, but H G intervened. "Save your denials, Mr Jenkins. I am aware that you came here today to make amends. But that is unimportant at this stage." She handed the suit of clothes, shirt and tie to George. "Go behind the screen and change, Mr Best, you are about to embark on a long journey."

George frowned. "Yes, to America. How did you know about that?"

"Never mind about that, I know a great deal about you, Mr Best, and where you fit into the scheme of things. But first, make yourself decent. You are about to meet your great-great-granddaughter."

George's eyebrows raised practically to his hairline. "What manner of lunacy is this? You people of society are as mad as hatters. I will change into your clothes, madam, but only because of the bounty that awaits me. And as soon as that occurs, I shall be off." He went behind the screen.

H G smiled. "Good, that's one thing arranged." She turned to Graham. "Now, good sir, I understand you have some photos you wish to give me, and a large sum of money so you can experience time travel."

It was Graham's turn to look astonished. "So you do have a time machine." He took a brown envelope from beneath his cloak and passed it to H G before turning to Samantha. "Clearly that polygraph is a lot of nonsense. Your lies, madam, were undetected."

Samantha was annoyed at being called a liar. "I can assure you, Mr Jenkins, self-proclaimed gentleman and scholar, that what I told you was indeed the truth." She turned to H G, maintaining her displeasure. "And you, my friend, have a great deal of explaining to do."

"Indeed I have, Samantha, and I will do so in due course. But first, there is a matter of business that I must conduct with Mr Jenkins."

Graham smirked, his eyebrow raised. "You consider yourself my equal in such matters, Miss Wells?"

H G's smile was sly. "Remember, sir, I am aware of the future, so I know where this is going."

Graham gasped. "What do mean? What else are you aware of?"

"What was the time this morning when you arrived at your warehouse to rescue Samantha?"

"Eleven-thirteen. How did you know I looked at my watch?"

"I was there, watching you."

Jenkins's cheeks bloomed with colour, and his startled eyes opened wide. "Good heavens. What else do you know about me?"

"I know how much you covet your upcoming time-travelling experience, so to save us both a lot of time, I have filled out a withdrawal form from your bank for the sum of fifty thousand guineas. All I need from you is to sign it, and to write and sign a letter of authorisation to accompany it."

Just then, George came from behind the screen looking resplendent in his new set of clothes. "Fifty thousand? Good Lord, that's far too much. I wouldn't know what to do with it."

"Only five thousand of that is yours, Mr Best, the remainder being split between your great-great-granddaughter and her future husband—a past scoundrel who has previously broken her heart but who has apparently mended his ways—and another as yet unconfirmed couple. Both pairs will start anew in another place and time for all but one of them."

George, at first, looked displeased, perhaps with the news that his future great-great-grandson-in-law was a scoundrel, but was smiling by the end of H G's statement.

"It is good to know that my actions will assist my descendant. Though this future husband of hers sounds like a ne'er-do-well."

Samantha intervened, expressing her approval of George's appearance. "Mr Best, I must say you look quite the gentleman."

"Aye, that I do. Although after today I am glad I am not truly of a gentleman's ranks, judging on the behaviour your lot has shown me."

Samantha laughed. "This is not our society's usual conduct, Mr Best. Believe it or not, we are normally quite reasoned and measured."

"Reasoned, you say, Mrs Rhodes? All this talk about time machines and meeting great-great-granddaughters begs one to differ, wouldn't you say?"

"But you yourself, Mr Best, have travelled with me through time." H G grinned.

He looked at H G incredulously. "Don't be ridiculous."

"How do you think I came across a set of clothes that fit your monstrous frame so well? You and I met with my tailor this very afternoon before returning to the present."

George looked down at his clothes, his arms bent, his face flummoxed.

H G continued. "You were dematerialised, your second self-bought back a few minutes earlier than when we left. Hence you have no recollection."

He paled, appearing to be completely lost.

Samantha broke the mood, and addressed H G sternly. "This dematerialising of people unbeknown to them, it is a circumstance that I wish to discuss with you."

"I would imagine you do. I will explain our particular situation when you and I leave with George later this afternoon for his trip to Australia."

"Australia? I am going to America."

"Are you, Mr Best? Let me ask you something, what is your trade? What do you hope to become in the new world?"

George pondered the question. "I have no trade. Well, certainly not a legal one."

"And this is exactly why you will board a ship bound for Melbourne this very day. Once on board, you will meet a chap by the name of Harry Fancy, a man who is an expert wine merchant looking for a new life for himself and his young wife in the Antipodes. All he needs is a backer, someone with ready funds to sponsor his venture, which he hopes to find upon his arrival. Instead, he will meet you on the voyage, thus beginning the successful firm of Best and Fancy, wine merchants."

George had a smile on his face that nearly burst. "And what will happen to me? Shall I marry?"

"Indeed, you shall, a woman by the name of Betty Jones, Harry Fancy's sister-in-law, who will be travelling with them to Melbourne. She too is a blond-haired, blue-eyed beauty like your great-great-granddaughter whom you are about to meet. Betty will love you with all her heart and bear you five healthy Australian children."

Graham Jenkins intervened. "This is all very well, Miss Wells, but this sum you propose I pay you is outrageous. What miracles shall I witness, the birth of Christ, his crucifixion?"

"Whatever your heart desires, good sir. But you should remember that as you were the architect of Samantha's misfortune, your payment should rightly be considered as recompense for your illegal act. A price I am sure you would prefer over a prison sentence."

Graham took a pen from his pocket and wrote and signed the letter of authority before signing the withdrawal form, passing them both to H G. "When shall we depart?"

"This very instant, my machine is parked in the back alley." She handed the withdrawal slip and letter to Samantha. "I shall be back shortly."

"Shortly?" Graham snorted. "I expected we would be gone for days, not minutes."

"As indeed we shall. But remember, good sir, we can return whenever we like."

"By Jove, you're right of course. I am finding it uncommonly difficult to grasp the intricacies of time travel."

"Don't worry, you will soon master it. However, I must ask you that, after experiencing our long and incredible journey, you keep it to yourself."

"I am to keep it a secret?"

"If you want to stay out of prison."

H G turned to Samantha. "And you, Samantha. Make sure you keep the secret of our time travel from innocent ears. George should meet with Jennifer and Shane privately, away from the other guests."

With that H G turned and left the room with Jenkins.

Chapter Eight

London 1898

Jennifer was beside herself with joy. She could not believe the change in Shane. He no longer needed to have *circumstances in his favour*, as he expressed, and he was willing to face what lay ahead without fear.

They walked back into the large parlour hand in hand and caused little or no reaction, which was understandable as no one from her past — which was, in fact, the future — was present. Simone was there with Katerina, and an attractive blonde and a large, fair-haired gentleman.

Simone introduced them both. "Jennifer and Shane, allow me to introduce Samantha."

The name of the woman surprised her. "Our abductee? You are returned?"

"Indeed, she is, and by the hero of the hour." Simone gestured to the man. "This is Mr George Best."

Jennifer's heart skipped a beat. *George Best? Surely not?* She was well aware of her ancestry, having had it investigated by a firm that specialised in such matters a few years ago. *He is fair and has blue eyes.* "Mr Best. Pleased to meet you. Let me guess, you're a wine merchant?"

"Not at this present moment, no." He smiled and seemed genuinely happy to meet her, his face beaming.

Jen was puzzled by the ambiguity of his response.

Before she could enquire further, Samantha intervened. "Perhaps we three should go outside into the garden. Shane can entertain Simone and Katerina."

Simone smiled cheerfully at Shane, taking Shane by the arm and ushering him toward one of the luxurious parlour chairs. "Indeed, it is. Let's the three of us sit together with a glass of wine while you tell us your story, Mr Courtney."

Jennifer shuddered at the thought of what Shane was about to tell Simone and Katerina, especially in light of his new-found honesty. But she was certain those two ladies, who harboured their own deep secret, would be as non-judgemental as anyone from this era could be. But for the moment, she was intrigued. Why had Samantha herded her and Mr Best off?

The three of them stepped out into the delightful garden. Samantha and Jennifer sat on the bench, while George stood with his hands behind, looking as though he were about to be judged for a heinous crime.

Samantha spoke first. "What I am about to tell you may shock you beyond belief, Miss Best, but the man before you is your great-great-grandfather."

Jennifer jumped out of the seat and embraced her large ancestor. "I knew it, I knew from the moment I saw you."

George returned Jennifer's warm embrace, smiling broadly as he held her to his now well-dressed chest.

Samantha seemed amazed. "You are not shocked, over-awed by the moment?"

Jennifer kept one arm around George's waist, who towered over her, looking up at him and then at Samantha. "Apart from the fact I have just travelled one hundred and twenty years back in time to a foreign land—which should inure any soul from any future surprises—I also am aware of my family tree. George here landed in Melbourne in December of this year."

Samantha sighed in relief.

George shrugged. "Apparently I am about to meet a

blond-haired beauty such as yourself on the voyage over. Her name is Betty, and Mr Fancy's sister-in-law."

"Betty, that's right, Betty Best, my great-great-grandmother," Jennifer squealed. "And Mr Fancy you say, of Best and Fancy wine merchants? Oh, this is so exciting. I should love to meet Betty."

George smiled. "So should I, Jennifer, but I will not do that until we sail."

Samantha had a mischievous smile on her face. "All is not lost. Perhaps we can have the Fancys pointed out to us on the docks. You must come with us, Jennifer, so you can say farewell to George, and you can at least look at her from afar, see her face."

Jennifer knew that her great-great-grandfather may be in London when she had left 2018 and had secretly hoped that she may meet him, but to see her great-great-grandmother, too, well that was amazing. "That would be wonderful, Samantha."

She put her free arm around Samantha's corseted waist, the feeling of which reminded her that she, too, was so adorned, something she realised she no longer noticed, its presence no longer an anomaly. They all embraced.

"You realise if I never kidnapped you, Samantha, I would never be going to Melbourne. And it is because of this, that you, Jennifer, exist." George's whimsical observation made her smile.

Then she paused, puzzled, looking from George to Samantha. "Kidnapped? I thought you were the saviour?"

George stepped back, gently holding her upper arms as he looked her squarely in the eye. "You should be aware I am not the man I seem. These clothes were given to me to replace my own rags, my trade that of a hired ruffian."

Jennifer started laughing.

"What's so funny?" he asked.

"The man I am about to marry was once the biggest scoundrel of all."

George frowned, somewhat grim. "I have heard such news."

"Have you? But the humorous thing about it is that he had me kidnapped, thrown in jail, then rescued just so he could own me."

Samantha gasped. "Good heavens. And you still want to marry him?"

"That was so long ago, one hundred and twenty years to be precise, and so far away. The man I am about to marry is no longer that man, and I know that for a fact. The point I am making is that he has changed, and so shall you, George." She embraced him once again, resting her head on his giant chest. "But it is funny that the men on either end of my family tree are both absolute rogues."

The three of them all laughed at this.

Samantha then addressed them with a serious expression. "H G has told me we must keep this matter of time travel between ourselves. You, George, Mr Jenkins, myself, and my husband, Peter, are the only ones from this present age aware of our secret."

Samantha then led them back into the house. "But now is a time for celebration. Georgina and Phyllis will be showered and redressed after their treatments, so they will be in high spirits plus their husbands, Derek and Pastor Miller, have been asked to attend. Add your friends Rebecca and Daria, and Peter and H G, together with us three and your future husband, Shane, and we are in for a wonderful party."

Jennifer could not wait.

George, on the other hand, looked a trifle concerned.

"What troubles you, George?" Jennifer asked.

"All this partying? I love my liquor, and I hope I don't

forget to board my ship."

"Don't worry about that, I'm a non-drinker so I'll keep you on the straight and narrow."

George looked amazed at this revelation. "A Best, an abstainer? I don't believe it."

They were all laughing as they entered the parlour, festivities already well underway.

H G took Jenkins out to the back and the awaiting DEMAT, moving across to the letterbox and opening the door. "In you go, Mr Jenkins."

Jenkins looked at her bewilderedly. "What on Earth, we shall barely fit."

"I need you to trust me, to take a leap of faith. You will be given what is rightfully yours, this I promise you."

Jenkins entered the tiny letterbox and was clearly overwhelmed by what he saw. "This space, how did you achieve this?"

"Samantha discovered the secret to dimensional transcendence when we travelled to the year twenty-seventy-eight. She is quite the genius."

Jenkins scanned the interior of the DEMAT with the wide-eyed look of a young child at an amusement park for the first time.

She handed him a small glass. "I need you to take this potion to inure you from the effects of time travel. Otherwise, you may end up insane."

Jenkins glared, doubtful. "*You* don't need to take it?"

"I have long since become immune to such effects. Drink that and we'll be on our way. Where would you like to go first?"

Jenkins drank the potion — unbeknown to him a hallucinogen — as H G took up her position at the console.

"God, that is bitter. I hope it does the trick."

"It will, trust me."

"Take me to the crucifixion, then to the building of the Sphinx. There is so much to see."

H G set her coordinates. She knew exactly where they were going and exactly the time to arrive there. She pressed the lever downwards and the DEMAT made its loud dematerialisation sound, this sudden noise and the hallucinogen causing Jenkins to cover his ears, his eyes expressing a fearsome dread.

"Are you okay, Mr Jenkins?" H G yelled amidst the din of the DEMAT.

Jenkins was screaming in absolute panic, his eyes opened wide with alarm.

The DEMAT ceased what must have seemed to Jenkins to be its thunderous whirring, the hallucinating effect of the drug clearly turning his journey into a nightmare.

"Get me out of here! Get me out of here!"

H G went across to him, taking him by the shoulders and leading him out of the DEMAT and onto the London alley. She took the distraught, but by then silent, Jenkins to a corner and peered around it. A carriage was coming down the street. *Perfect.*

H G waited until the carriage pulled up and a tall man in a black cloak alighted. She gently guided Jenkins toward the man who was looking at his watch, as did she. *Eleven-thirteen, exactly as he had said.* She whispered into the terrified Jenkins's ear. "Go to the man you see Graham, he is a nice man, he will help you." H G watched from the shadows as the artificially distressed Graham stumbled across to the man. Then, just as he was about to reach him, Jenkins disappeared into a puff of nothingness.

The man in the cloak turned around, his face in absolute fear. It was Jenkins, about to enter his warehouse and discover that Samantha was gone.

But H G wasn't finished with Jenkins. She knew she had to prevent him from turning up at the party or else she would have created a time loop where she and Jenkins would be continually playing out this charade. Pulling the bludgeon out from her pocket, she crept up behind Jenkins and hit him as hard as she could, knocking him unconscious. She then knelt and extracted the brown envelope with the photos from his jacket.

Checking quickly, H G saw there was no one present, so she dragged Jenkins's unconscious body down to the mattress in the cellar where Samantha had been held. She looked at him and smiled, then walked back up the stairs, locking the doors to both the cellar and the warehouse before returning to the DEMAT. She then set her coordinates to return to the alley a few minutes after she had left with Jenkins, making sure she did not dematerialise herself. She would come back for Jenkins the next day, rescuing him from his cellar, well after George Best had left for Australia, and well after she had dealt with some other important matters.

Without the photos, Jenkins would have nothing to support his ridiculous time-travel claims. Jenkins would assume that his fellow kidnapper had snatched Samantha and had knocked him out and left him there. H G would confirm this when she came to collect him tomorrow, saying that George had told her where to find him. When Jenkins discovered that fifty thousand guineas had been withdrawn from his account by a large, well-dressed gentleman with a letter from himself authorising it, he would be puzzled. But because of his involvement in the kidnapping, he would have to remain silent, no doubt putting it all down to experience in the cold light of day. Meanwhile, her main purpose of getting Jenkins off her tail would have been realised.

When the DEMAT arrived back in the alley, H G was

mightily pleased with herself and her clever manoeuvrings.

Simone looked around at the throng assembled in her parlour. It was a hive of activity, people from all corners of the globe smiling and talking incessantly. *Such warmth, such humanity.* Peter had introduced Daria and Rebecca to her, more visitors from Australia, or so she assumed by their accents and also their strange, concise way of speaking. It was as if they, along with Shane and Jennifer, were in a hurry, their speech no longer an art form but a means to an end. She prayed neither she nor her friends would ever talk in such a manner.

By the time H G entered the room, everyone was there. Everyone that is, except for her friend Gigi who was over from Paris, visiting her and Katerina. Gigi Chevalier was nocturnal, never rising before noon, her employment as a bar manager in the cultural centre of Paris more or less necessitating her sleeping habits.

Simone excused herself from her guests before going upstairs, knocking on the door of one of the bedrooms before entering. Her and Katerina's home above the institute was extremely spacious. Their bedroom was the largest, complete with an en suite, with a common bathroom serving the two guestrooms.

Gigi was already up, applying her make up in front of the mirror. Although Gigi herself was of a sapphic nature, Simone and she had never been romantically involved. Simone's sadomasochistic needs were foreign to Gigi's romantic spirit. They had met at Gigi's bar, a bohemian place where artists, poets, and writers of all sexual preferences gathered. It was a gay place, far removed from the rigid, repressed society of London's elite, where Simone had found herself domiciled. Because of this, it was good for her, Simone a Parisian herself, to make contact with Gigi on a regular basis, keeping her in touch with her roots.

Simone smiled at Gigi as she sat in front of the mirror expertly applying her makeup. Although her English compatriots never used cosmetics, Gigi was uninhibited by their custom. She was an utterly feminine soul, her outfits always graceful, flowing affairs, dresses that highlighted her slender, yet curvy frame. Simone thought of her as delightful, her makeup understated and refined, an urbane woman of absolute class.

Gigi spoke without turning her face from the mirror, applying the finishing touches of her cherry-coloured lipstick. "There seems to be a lot of noise coming from below, my darling, what is the occasion?"

"Samantha, Peter's wife, has been rescued from her abduction. Her saviour, a Mr Best, an impoverished soul, is being feted and rewarded, myself and Katerina contributing to his payment. There are all manner of people there, even Australians, would you believe, including a most robust individual, a Rebecca Browning, a police inspector called in to assist."

"Robust, you say?" Gigi rubbed her lace-gloved finger across Simone's cheek as she walked past, smiling her bright red lips. "I look forward to meeting *her*."

Georgina Miller, wife of the popular and liberal, Pastor Miller, and Mrs Phyllis Jones, wife of the extremely wealthy Mr Derek Jones, showered together after completing their four-hour treatments. Treatments that were not only accepted by their husbands but encouraged by them, both men eager to ensure their wives' hysterias never returned.

She and Phyllis were both from well-respected society families and had first met at Doctor Peter Rhodes's institute where they were both cured of their respective maladies. Phyllis's was ennui, or chronic boredom, while Georgina was suffering from a deep anxiety, both of them cured by experiencing their first orgasm. Something that, prior to entering the institute, neither ever thought possible, having been taught by their society that women *could not experience such physical events.*

Georgina was well aware that all of Doctor Rhodes's patients were cured in the same manner. Apparently, Peter was conscious of the fact that his society's rigid morality and behavioural rules had caused a widespread sexual repression amongst the female gender, resulting in an epidemic of so-called *hysteria*. Consequently, his business was thriving, its secretive methods of tight restraints, sensory deprivation, and vaginal massaging both enjoyed and adored by his clientele.

Georgina and Phyllis had just completed their biannual, four-hour sexual maintenance at Simone and Katerina's London branch of the institute, a service that naturally was exclusive to their establishment. Subsequently, both women were highly enthused as they showered together.

Georgina, in particular, was extremely pleased with herself, having experienced three separate, tumultuous orgasms—which was her norm—during her confinement. "How was it for you today, Phyllis?"

"Oh, absolutely marvellous. I once again achieved a triple, which I only do when under Simone's wondrous restraints, followed by a longer, more peaceful orgasm. What about yourself?" The normal, rules of polite, timid conversation had been cast to the breeze by the two good friends within the institute's uninhibited walls.

Georgina looked at Phyllis, a woman probably ten years her senior and the only married woman Peter had ever treated. "A triple, again? I remain in wonder of you, Phyllis.

I, myself, have never had such a pleasure."

"Oh, I wouldn't worry too much about that, Peter ensures me it's a most rare occurrence."

"Oh, I am far from worried, madam." She smiled as she sponged her voluptuous frame. "I managed my usual three singular explosions, all of which sent me into a Shangri la of pure rapture, the like of which I only achieve while under either Simone or Katerina's care."

They dried themselves before dressing back into their normal walking suits, having experienced their sexual maintenance in their emerald green institute uniforms, which would be cleaned and ready for them at their next visit. Both women were tying their hair into elaborate chignons which they would then pin their bonnets on before adorning their finely textured gloves.

"Katerina informed me there was a party going on, Georgina. Apparently, Samantha was kidnapped yesterday and miraculously returned today."

"Yes, she told me the same thing as she untied me. It is the first I knew about it, as well."

"Our delightful hostesses—who, along with our darling husbands, are out there waiting for us—probably didn't want to ruin our experiences. They are so mindful of us, such thoughtfulness."

They both looked at their images with approval then, taking their parasols, they moved toward the parlour and the celebrations.

H G stood in front of the assembled guests, tinkling a glass to draw their attention. Eventually, the hubbub died down, and she addressed them in a loud, clear tone.

"Ladies and gentlemen. If I could have your attention for just a short while. I have some brief announcements to make and then we can all resume the festivities."

The assembled guests all turned their attention to her.

"As you are aware, our delightful and clever friend, Samantha Rhodes, was returned to us today, courtesy of a gentleman by the name of George Best."

She paused a moment as the crowd cheered.

"If you could step forward please, George." She waited as George sheepishly moved forward to stand beside her. "Samantha and her good friends, Simone and Katerina, were going to reward George with a substantial bounty of five thousand guineas. However, I am pleased to announce that we have received the funds from a generous donor who wishes to remain anonymous."

Once again, everyone cheered, raising their glasses in unison.

"George will use the money to embark on an adventure of a lifetime, deciding to migrate to Melbourne, Australia."

Derek, Phyllis's husband, piped up. "There are a few of the antipodeans amongst us today, perhaps they can give him a heads-up of what it's like."

H G doubted that very much, seeing they were from 2018, far removed from 1898 Melbourne, although the gold rush had made it a very rich place and one of the top ten cities in the world at that time. She continued. "I understand Samantha and Jennifer will be accompanying George to the docks presently. So please, make your selves known to our honoured guest before he leaves."

Jennifer took her secret ancestor by the arm and walked him around, introducing him, and herself at times, for she, too, had yet to meet some of the guests.

It was then that H G noticed Simone coming down the stairs with a most delightful creature on her arm, Simone's dear friend, Gigi Chevalier. She immediately looked across the room at Rebecca Downing and saw her staring at the new arrival, her mouth agape.

Stopping on the second to last step of the staircase, Simone, with her usual flourish, loudly announced Gigi to the party. "Charming people, allow me to introduce you all to one of my dearest friends who has recently arrived from Paris. Miss Gigi Chevalier. Please make her welcome."

Everyone cheered a loud welcome, and Josephine passed Gigi a glass of champagne as she mingled amongst the guests.

What manner of a creature is this? Rebecca could not believe her eyes as she gazed at Simone's companion standing on the stairwell. *It is like she has stepped out of some movie set.* Unlike the rest of her female companions, Gigi's black hair was cropped, and she was wearing a tight-fitting, flowing, full-length cream gown. Her elegant neck was captured by the delicate material of the high collar that highlighted her corseted, slim, feminine frame. Loose fitting, full-length sleeves ran down to wrists that were cuffed by four buttons, the narrowness of the gown's cuffs highlighting the delicacy of its wearer. Rebecca was enraptured.

Her heart began to beat a thousand miles an hour as she saw Simone and the captivating Gigi being pointed in her direction by Jennifer, the both of them smiling as they walked toward her. *Be still my beating heart.* Did she really just think that? Rebecca Downing considered herself the most pragmatic, methodical, least romantic soul on the planet, and here she was behaving like a schoolgirl. But try as she may, she could not help herself. Her heart continued to beat at an alarming rate, and her knees very nearly buckled as the beauty drew closer.

"Rebecca Browning? My name is Simone. I am, along with my lifetime companion Katerina, your hostess today.

Allow me to introduce you to my dear friend and fellow Parisian, Gigi Chevalier."

Rebecca gazed into Gigi's brown eyes, the depth and meaning of which enveloped her soul, turning her into a tongue-tied mess. She merely smiled, barely managing to do that as the beautiful young lady proffered her finely-laced hand for Rebecca to kiss. Rebecca hesitantly, carefully, followed the young enchantress's direction, softly kissing her hand, this tiniest of actions causing her body to be invaded by a thousand butterflies, once again sending her into a spin. *Jesus, what is happening to me?*

Rebecca turned to her hostess, slightly confused that such romantic behaviour between two females caused little or no reaction. "Your guests, Simone, won't they be offended? Peter tells me they remain unaware of your own attachment."

"Oh, Gigi is a Continental, and as such, they regard her behaviour as outside their realm and indeed, are quite accommodating of it."

Then Gigi spoke. Her mellow, alto tone combined with her French accent to send Rebecca onto an even higher plane. "Simone tells me you are Australian." She gave Rebecca a look that so bordered on incitement it would be considered a crime back in her modern world. "I have never met someone from your faraway land. You must tell me all about it."

Simone's confident voice broke the spell that Rebecca found herself under. "I shall leave you two alone."

Finally, Rebecca was able to utter a word, turning to Simone. "Yes, yes, of course. Thank you, Simone, nice to have met you."

Simone smiled as she walked away, blending into the crowd, which had become a meaningless background to Rebecca, her attention unable to be drawn away from the magnetism of her entrancing companion.

Mentally shaking herself back to some form of reality, she

returned her gaze to Gigi, attempting to regain her assertiveness. "Come on, let's sit down. I am sure we have lots to tell each other about our very different cultures." She took Gigi's arm, guiding her to the two-seater settee in a silent corner of the room.

Gigi smiled cheekily. "Commanding, I like that in a woman."

Well, you'll love me. But despite her bravado, she was far from her typical self-confidence as they sat down, staring at one another. Rebecca had never felt like this toward another person. She had had affairs, not many, her career taking precedence over all else in her life, but this girl was something else. "Jesus, you are so fucking beautiful. I just want to eat you up."

Rebecca couldn't believe she blurted that out, and it appeared to startle the worldly-wise Parisian, as well.

Gigi's eyes widening for the briefest of moments before returning to her former poise. "You are speaking to a woman from the Continent, lovely lady. We prefer our meals to be introduced by an entree."

Why did I say that? What in the fuck is wrong with me? I have no fucking idea what I am doing with this ethereal creature.

Gigi must have sensed her dilemma, stroking Rebecca's cheek with her finely adorned hand as she smiled with the friendliest of expressions. "Do not worry, I am not offended. Au contraire, my strong friend, au contraire."

Rebecca knew enough French to know that meant *on the contrary* and she was intensely relieved. Courting this delightful soul was like manoeuvring around a minefield for her, such was her feeling of inadequacy. But once again Gigi must have sensed her disquiet, coming to her rescue, rubbing her hand gently against Rebecca's tailored upper sleeve. *God, her touch is electrifying.*

"Please, be yourself. It is that person I seek to know and to whom I was attracted across the crowded room. Clearly, you are a strong, assertive, confident woman who knows what she wants and how to get it. I am not after another version of myself. I have had such women and I end up either bored, depressed, or both. I want someone with female strength, who can take me on a different journey, to a place I've never been."

Female strength? I can supply that. Rebecca started to relax, any considerations of confected femininity discarded by Gigi's meaningful words. "Thank Christ. I have never been so frightened in my life."

"A police inspector, frightened? I doubt that."

"Don't get me wrong, beautiful lady. I'm frightened of no bastard. But the fear of displeasing you, it was turning me into a wimp."

They both laughed loudly, their relationship on its way, and beginning on a firm, honest footing.

CHAPTER NINE

Scotland 1310

Simon lay on a bed in a rough, fourteenth-century Scottish prison beside four of the most brutal men he had ever encountered. He had been thrown in there by Robert the Bruce who was enraged that Simon had refused to join his army in his battle against the English invaders.

He recalled his first meeting with King Robert after H G had departed in her DEMAT, leaving him there. Simon was by then unrestrained and had been fed by his Scottish host who was in awe of H G's mystical appearances and departures, viewing her as an oracle. Consequently, he was elated when she had left Simon with him, referring to him as *a fearsome warrior* and the *Scottish nation's saviour*.

"So what is your name?" His English was excellent, which was a blessing.

Simon wondered if he should call himself Jack the Ripper. *No, his place will be recorded in history in another time and place, this adventure entirely separate.* "Simon Lewis."

Robert the Bruce laughed. "Simon the Lewis? What does that mean?"

Simon ignored him, getting to the point instead. "I am here to kill some people, slit their throats."

"Your tongue, it is strange. From where do you hail?"

Simon was about to reply with Australia when he realised that no such country existed in these times. "Austria. Now, with regards to your warfare, what have you got planned?"

"Hmm, Simon the Austrian." He appeared to reflect on this. "We march on the English army shortly."

That sounds fucked. "Army? What are the odds?"

"They outnumber us heavily, but our bravery will win through."

"Fuck that, mate. You can stick that up your arse. That's no way to win a war."

That had led to Simon being left in a cell at night, defence-less, and supposedly about to sleep beside four murderous barbarians, brutes so unruly they were called the *uncontrollable* and locked away by their own people.

One of his new companions was a giant of a man, at least two metres tall with the broadest of frames. *Wee Michael,* King Robert had called him. The man had smiled at Simon with his filthy, sparsely-teethed grin when Simon had been deposited into their cell.

But Simon had come prepared. After dining with King Robert, he had kept the wooden spoon, breaking it apart in a moment alone, and, using his teeth, shaping one end into the sharpest point he could manage. A shiv, as they had called it in prison.

He lay there, his face toward a brick wall with his back turned to his foes, pretending to be asleep as he awaited their undoubted attack. Then it came. He heard one of them approach, and with the speed of a cobra, he turned and sprang at his assailant, stabbing him in the eye. It was the giant, Wee Michael. The man screamed in agony as he lurched around the cell, crashing into the walls before falling down, crumpling into a foetal position on the floor, his hand over his eye that had blood gushing from it. Simon stood in a crouched position, brandishing his weapon as he glared at the other three men, all of whom stood with their hands up as if in surrender, clearly in dread of his crazed, maniacal presence.

Out of the corner of his eye, Simon saw the guard rush to the barred cell, calling out something that was indistinguishable, and another man joined him instantly. They spoke amongst themselves, Simon hearing the words *Robert and Bruce* mentioned.

One of the guards left as Simon reviewed his situation. Wee Michael had calmed down, one of the other men covering his damaged eye with a rag. Simon remained poised, his body still in a crouched, defensive position. His nerves were on edge, his warring instincts ever-ready, though once again his murderous heart was unmoved. *Fuck you, you cunts, Jack the fucking Ripper is amongst you.*

There was a commotion outside the cell, then a group of men entered, one of which was Robert the Bruce. He looked amazed and puzzled. He barked a command, and one of the guards opened the cell.

Simon glared at the guard, ready to kill him if necessary.

King Robert spoke out, easing the tension all around. "Simon the Austrian, you are quite the dilemma. I thought you a coward. Clearly, this is not the case. Why did you refuse to join my army?"

"Because it is fucking stupid. That's not the way to win a war against a stronger force. You need to use guerrilla tactics, hit and run."

"Is that so?" Robert the Bruce stared at him before relaxing his jaw and smiling. "Let us start again. I apologise for misunderstanding you. Come, sit with me and drink."

Simon scrutinised him, seeing if he was on the level, while at the same time keeping his attention firmly on his barbaric cellmates. He edged toward the door, only putting his shiv into his jacket pocket when he was outside, and the door locked.

King Robert put his arm around Simon's shoulder, which he regarded with suspicion as he walked with him up the stairs and into his chambers, the other men, bar one, leaving them alone.

The king introduced his companion. "This is Aidan Alleyn. He is Irish, and he hates the English more than we do. Aidan, this is Simon the Austrian, a most fearsome warrior."

Aidan held his hand out for Simon to shake, which Simon ignored. "So fucking what. Who is he to me?"

"He is to be your interpreter. He speaks fluent English. If you are to lead a band of my men in attack as you say, you will need him."

Simon looked Aidan up and down, before deciding to shake his hand. He was still on edge, ready to pounce at the slightest provocation.

Aidan smiled, his soft voice made even more mellow by his Irish brogue. "Calm down, my fighting friend. Let's the three of us sit and talk, have some wine and discuss your strategy."

Simon continued to view them both with suspicion before following their lead and sitting. The Irishman poured him a glass of red wine, but he refused. The last time he had partaken he had ended up in irons, delivered to his present location by H G.

"This hit and run warfare, what was it you called it?" Aidan asked.

"Guerrilla."

"How do you propose it would work?"

"I'll do better than that. You give me four men and I will show you how it works."

Robert the Bruce intervened. "Four of my men? I cannot spare the one."

"No, not your men, those men." Simon pointed toward the cell, toward the uncontrollables.

Robert the Bruce looked at him as if he were insane. "Are you insane, man? They will cut your throat the first chance they get, especially after what you did to Wee Michael."

"But that's where you are wrong." Simon knew better. He knew what type of men they were. They were like him, cold-blooded killers unable to fit into a rational society. And as such, they were ruled by the only thing they understood and respected . . . violence. He pointed to Aidan. "You come with me. I will tell them what they want to hear."

Simon sat in the cell with the uncontrollable four, Michael's eye covered with a bandage. Through Aidan, Simon spoke to them all. "Follow me and you will be out of this place. But not as fugitives, as warriors, free to kill hundreds of English souls as you roam the untamed highlands where you belong."

He watched as the four talked amongst themselves, but he knew what their answer would be. They, like him, were put on this Earth to kill, their crazed souls unable to exist peacefully unless their bloodlust was satisfied. He was expecting no loyalty, just a mutual dependence on each other. As long as they stayed with him under Robert the Bruce's favour, they would be free to follow their true destinies, and during this time of war, be lauded for it.

He observed them with interest, as the four men, apparently all from some wild, highland clan, talked with Aidan. Then suddenly, in the middle of their conversation, they all stopped and turned to him with startled expressions before resuming their conversation with Aidan, their utterances far more animated than before. Finally, the discussion ended, all four of the uncontrollables nodding their heads and looking at Simon with reverence.

What in the fuck is going on here?

Aidan turned to him. "It seems a fearless warrior such as yourself has been prophesied amongst their clan for centuries, so when I told them you arrived in a strange manner from the heavens, they became certain of who you are. They now view you as some supernatural being, sent from the

Gods. They would follow you to their deaths if you so desire it."

Fucking superstitious bastards. But Simon was fine with that. Loyalty is a commodity to be used. Shane had shown him that back in their world. He scowled at Aidan. "You tell them that no one will be going to their deaths, except their enemies. As long as they follow my instructions to the letter."

He gave the men a thumbs up as Aidan passed on his words. The four men smiled and put their thumbs up in response.

Simon took Aidan aside. "You will accompany us until I learn the language. Also, I want you to occasionally report to King Robert to tell him of our successes. Once he sees what we achieve, he will organise his whole army this way. Soon he will have his enemy on its knees, seeking peace."

London 1898

Shane could not believe how fulfilled he felt as he watched Jennifer introduce her great-great-grandfather to the guests. *She is such a delight, and she loves me. Me.* He could not believe it.

Then he acted as he had never before, compulsively. Without forethought, he walked across to Jennifer and knelt before her. The crowd moved back as Shane looked up at Jennifer, prepared to take the biggest risk of his life, a public rejection. But he no longer cared about such things. His desire for Jen was such a force that nothing else mattered. "Jennifer Best, you are the very reason I exist. I could not imagine life without you. Please, my darling, will you become my wife?"

The throng stood in silence, all awaiting Jennifer's reply.

Shane's heart was beating a hundred miles an hour as he looked up at Jennifer. Her beautiful blue eyes shifting from one side to the other as she examined him.

She pulled him up and took him to the side, whispering for only him to hear. "Shane, as much as I want to, I cannot marry you, you are a fugitive. As soon as we return to Melbourne, you will be imprisoned."

Shane's mind was racing, searching for a solution. Then it came, in a form he could never have dreamt of.

H G joined them, her attention on Jennifer. "You must follow your heart on this, Jennifer. Your destiny lies in another time and place from this one and indeed from your old life."

"What do you mean?" Jennifer asked.

H G handed Shane a book, *Shares and Property movements from 1885-1895*. She patted the book and leant in closer. "This, along with the twenty-five thousand guineas, which we will soon collect from Mr Jenkins's bank, will set you, Jennifer and your children up for life."

Shane examined the small, brown book, then peered at H G, confused. "I don't understand? What good is this?"

"As of this moment, it is of little or no value, but in the right circumstances it would be priceless to a man of your talent."

Jennifer's eyes were full of tears as she asked, "H G, what are you saying?"

H G raised her eyebrows and chuckled. "Well, do you want to marry him?"

Jennifer looked at Shane, her expression one of bewilderment, his fear nearly overwhelming him. Her gaze continued to dart across Shane's face as if searching for something.

She turned back to H G. "What are you proposing I do?"

"If you accept his proposal, and only because you love him with all of your heart I must stress, then I have a solution to the problem of Shane's imprisonment. So make your decision based on your sentiment, not your reason."

Jennifer stared at him again, her eyes expressing the deepest of affection. "I do love you with all of my heart, Shane Courtney. Therefore, I unconditionally accept your proposal, though God only knows where it may lead us."

Shane, lost in euphoria from her words, was pulled back to the present as the assembly, though unable to hear their words, apparently saw Jennifer's positive response, and all of them cheered as one.

He cried unashamedly, as he gently held his beloved's face, examining her amazing blue eyes before kissing her as tenderly and gratefully as he had ever kissed anybody before.

H G interrupted the revelry. "The first thing we must do is get you married before we send you off on your strangest of honeymoons." She turned to the crowd and grinned. "Ladies and gentlemen, we have a wedding on our hands."

The rest of the gathering quickly regained their composure as they rushed across to congratulate him and Jennifer. Shane felt overwhelmed by it all, as he was sure Jen was, but never before had he felt so joyful. *Shit, she's going to marry me. I can't fucking believe it.*

As he accepted everyone's good wishes, he looked across at his wonderful bride-to-be and then at H G who smiled knowingly back at him. *What has she got planned for us?*

H G approached Pastor Miller, Georgina's husband, extracting some forms from her pocket. "I have here the necessary papers to legalise their nuptials, all I need is for you to conduct the ceremony."

Rather than looking surprised at this, Pastor Miller, whose reputation as a liberal soul preceded him, smiled warmly at H G. "Ever prepared I see, Miss Wells. Find me a bible and we shall proceed. As a recently married man myself, I am in no doubt of the urgency of their marriage, their love for each other manifest."

So with that H G had arranged the pair's wedding, which proceeded without drama, George Best giving the bride away and the festive assembly giving the happy couple three loud cheers.

She then pulled the couple aside, addressing Shane first. "That book I gave you." Shane pulled it out from his pocket. "You asked me of what good it is?"

"I did, and I still do."

"Tell me, Shane, of what benefit would it be, along with twenty-five thousand guineas, to a man of your skills in eighteen-eighty-five London?"

Jennifer gasped. "That is your solution, to send us back there?"

"It is."

Jennifer and Shane looked to each other before smiling and embracing.

"Shane, we can do it, build a life together."

"We can, plus you get to stay in your corsetry." Shane wiggled his eyebrows, and the two laughed as they continued to embrace, gazing affectionately at each other.

H G interrupted their bliss. "There is, however, one stipulation of the dowager's that is uncompromising"

Jennifer was the one to express their concern. "And what is that?"

"That Daria must accompany you. About this the dowager is unequivocal."

They both smiled as Jennifer once again spoke on the newlyweds' behalf. "We wouldn't have it any other way."

"Absolutely," Shane affirmed.

"Good." H G then thought about what else she had to do, to set everything in train. "I will leave it to you two to inform Daria. Do you envisage any problems, Jennifer?"

"With Daria? God no, she loves an adventure."

"Yes, well once you have that sorted could you send her to me. Then you, Samantha, and I must be off. We have a most important engagement to fulfil at the docks." She looked across at George who was fully engaged with Simone, Katerina, and to H G's absolute delight, an arm-in-arm Rebecca and Gigi. *Hmm, that seems to be going well.* But most importantly, George was without a glass in his hand. *Good, I need him sober. He has an important task to fulfil.*

Daria crossed the room toward H G, thrilled with the news she had received from Jennifer and Shane. She was glad H G wanted to speak with her for she had something urgent to ask her.

As she approached, H G smiled. "Daria, just the person I wanted to see. Are you happy with Jennifer and Shane's proposal?"

"Of course, I would never leave her side." She wondered how best she should proceed with her next enquiry, deciding in the end to just express herself honestly. If it came across as selfish or egocentric, then so be it. "H G, what is my purpose in all of this? Will my destiny be fulfilled?"

She was taken aback by the intensity H G displayed.

"Yours, Daria, is the most important of all. Without it, nothing would eventuate. Believe me."

Daria was excited. She knew she was acting self-centred, but it was heartening to know that her presence was vital in all of this. She was content with H G's explanation, not needing to know where her destiny lay. She had a part to play, an important one, and with that, she felt satisfied, at peace with herself.

CHAPTER TEN

London 1898

Jennifer stood with Samantha and George at the docks, waiting to see George off. She admired Samantha greatly. She was a woman of outstanding talent, and in keeping with her times, conducted herself with absolute charm and grace. Indeed, as had everyone she had met at their wedding party, as it had turned out to be. She was so looking forward to spending her life amidst such elegance with her handsome man. *Eighteen-eighty-five, I wonder what it will be like?*

Samantha had conducted herself superbly at the bank, the large amount of money passed to her without concern due to her standing as a respected society gentlewoman. She had given George his five thousand and Jennifer her twenty-five, retaining the other twenty for a future cause of which Jennifer had no idea, H G apparently the only person in possession of that particular knowledge.

Jennifer was looking amongst the crowd that had assembled in front of the steamer, trying to catch a glimpse of Betty Fancy, her great-great-grandmother, but it was so crowded it was nigh on impossible. But not for George who towered over everyone else.

He smiled at her. "Looking for your Betty, aye?"

"I am yes."

"Well, I think I may have spotted her, a little tintype of her great-great-granddaughter. Blonde, beautiful, and full of smiles. What say we all go across and introduce ourselves?"

Jennifer was beside herself. *Could it be possible, that she could meet her other ancestor?* But how would George manage it? After all, he was no genius. "What are you going to say to them, George?"

"I am not the simpleton I appeared to be amongst the gentry, Jennifer. Out here I am amongst my own kind. How do you think I survived for so long doing the things I do?" He looked across at Samantha. "The two of you just follow my lead, all right?"

Samantha smiled, admiration shining in her eyes. "Once again I find myself in your capable hands, Mr Best. Pray, show us the way."

Jennifer was curious about the familiarity displayed by the pair. But on reflection, they had spent some time together, and it was clear they had developed a bond, one that might even be described as a friendship.

She was walking alongside George and Samantha across the docks when the woman in question came into view. Her heart seemed to stop as she caught sight of her great-great-grandmother. Betty was as George had described, a smaller, younger version of herself.

Jennifer fought for calm, eager not to draw any unnecessary attention. She watched George as they neared their quarry, eager to see how her great-great-grandfather would handle himself.

George walked straight across to the man standing next to Betty. "Harry Fancy?"

The young man turned to George looking up at his massive frame. "It is indeed. And your name, good sir?"

"Allow me to introduce myself and my friends. My name is George Best, and this is my niece Jennifer and her friend Mrs Samantha Rhodes."

His niece? Clever move Uncle *George.*

Harry shook George's hand and nodded his acknowledgement of Jennifer and Samantha before introducing his companions. "This is my wife, Katherine, and her younger sister, Betty Jones."

Jennifer nodded to her great-great-grandmother, making sure she smiled warmly and equally at both women as she acknowledged the introduction. *What a delightful creature.* Jennifer's heart was tingling, enthralled by her surreal situation.

Samantha handled the pleasantries on their behalf, clearly aware of the momentous occasion it must be for Jennifer. "How do you do?"

Harry Fancy turned to George. "How was it you came across my name, good sir?"

"A friend of mine, a business acquaintance, alerted me to the fact that you would be on board my ship. It seems we may have mutual interests that could be of benefit to us both."

"Is that so?"

"Yes. I understand you are an expert in wine and that you are venturing to far-off Melbourne in search of your riches?"

"Indeed, I am. But of what interest is that to you?"

"I am looking for a business to invest in as I make my way to the new world, and you have come highly recommended. So there you have it. I have the capital you need, and you have the expertise I lack. What say you to a partnership, good fellow?"

Fancy appeared amazed. "Such serendipity, I am dumbfounded." His expression quickly changed to one of complete seriousness. "You mentioned capital. Are you aware of the considerable outlay to establish oneself as a wine merchant?"

"I have no idea. Pray, inform me."

"Well, it depends on the size of course. But even for a small beginning, it would cost upwards of five hundred guineas."

"And what of a large enterprise? How much are we looking at there?"

Fancy was shocked, looking at George dubiously. "Surely you jest sir. You know naught of me."

"But that is where you are wrong, Harry, you don't mind if I call you Harry?"

"Not all . . . George."

"In fact, I know a great deal about you, good sir, and your skill at your trade, and my source is impeccable." He turned to Samantha. "Would not you agree with me, Mrs Rhodes, an impeccable source?"

"Impeccable indeed, Mr Best. Indisputably."

"Well, if you wanted to have a good go at this, something in the order of three thousand guineas would be needed."

George put his enormous hand out for the slightly built Harry to shake. "Done."

Harry shook his hand, his expression absolutely flummoxed.

George then stealthily pulled his money out, careful to keep its presence away from prying eyes. "Just to show you, Harry, that I am indeed a man of substance. Now, what cabin are you in?"

"Cabin? Oh no sir, we are not in a cabin. We are below decks."

"Ridiculous. I will not allow my future partner and two such charming ladies to travel under such circumstances. Samantha, you know best how to handle such matters. Let's get the Fancys and the delightful Miss Jones into a cabin adjoining my own. We shall spend the voyage getting to know each other in comfort and style."

Jennifer was flabbergasted. Gone was the bumbling, inelegant giant who looked so out of place in Simone and Katerina's parlour, replaced by a man confident in his abilities.

She thought about Shane and his confidence and worldly charm. *Both sides of the family. What hope have our children got?*

Samantha replied to George's request, smiling gracefully. "That will be no problem, George. I shall arrange it with the captain. And I have arranged your luggage as well."

George looked surprised. "My luggage?"

"Certainly. H G has organised it, your bags befitting a businessman of your stature."

Jennifer had kept her eyes on Betty during the intercourse between George and Harry. At first, she seemed unimpressed by George, but as the sincerity and the generosity of his offer unfolded, Jennifer could see she was taken by his standing.

Samantha and Jennifer hugged their companions as they prepared to leave the decks of the giant steamer. When it came to hugging Betty, Jennifer gave her an extra squeeze as she whispered in her ear. "You look after my Uncle George, Betty, won't you? He is a good man."

Betty glanced at her somewhat bewilderedly, before smiling warmly as she whispered her reply. "I doubt I have ever met a man less in need of looking after in my life, but if your entreaty is of the manner in which I imagine, I agree with you. He seems a fine, jolly man, one that any girl would love to know better."

Jennifer could not help herself, squeezing her once again, this time with tears in her eyes. "Good luck, Betty."

With that she walked down the gangplank, Samantha following her until they stood together, waving at their friends as the ship began its long journey to her land, a land she now knew she would never see again.

Samantha must have noticed her sentimentality, putting her arm around her. "Such an emotional experience, I can barely envision what is going on in that mind of yours. To meet and embrace your forebearers, I imagine it is quite overwhelming."

Jennifer put her arm around Samantha, smiling at her warmly in response, wiping away her tears as she again waved goodbye. "It is a bit, but it is also exciting. Plus, Shane and I will be leaving tomorrow, off to start our own new life."

"Really, where to?"

"It is more when, than where, Samantha. H G is taking us to eighteen-eighty-five."

"Is she now?" She waved at George and his new companions as she talked. "These journeys of H G's, I have one in particular of my own to discuss with her."

Jennifer looked at her in amazement. *Where in the world would she and Peter want to go to? They have it all, right where they were.*

Jennifer sighed in relief. The party was over. Pastor Miller and Georgina, and Derek and Phyllis Jones, had returned to their homes, none the wiser about H G's time travels. She and Shane were about to spend the first night of their honeymoon at the main institute, a country manor, *the kinky couple* to be taken there by the institute's manservant George in the institute's carriage.

Jennifer had been presented with an emerald green institute uniform by Peter and Samantha, which she was now wearing.

"Christ, this is so beautiful. Who designed it?" she asked as she admired herself in the mirror.

Samantha replied with obvious pride. "My clever husband."

Jennifer smiled. "You have quite the eye, Peter."

Peter nodded his thanks. "We will leave you both together. Samantha and I remember our own first night, which also began with a carriage ride to the institute. It was amazing as I am sure yours will be." Peter took Samantha's waist, clearly happy to have her by his side again, kissed her lightly on the lips, then bid them farewell. "Enjoy yourselves. George and Mary will look after your every need while at the manor, which is beautifully appointed."

Alone together, at last, Shane stood a few metres away, clearly admiring what he was seeing as Jennifer continued watching her movements in the mirror.

Her uniform was a superbly tailored, double-breasted suit, its jacket extending to just below her buttocks, with an elegantly draped full-length skirt. A stiff white upturned collar with a striped black and white tie together with a boater hat, gloves, and black, pointy-toed ankle boots complemented her outfit while underneath a tight corset clung to her exquisitely. Jennifer was in heaven, the moisture of joy appearing the moment she began to don her uniform.

Then, of course, there was the carriage ride, which would take two hours.

Shane had been equipped with many coils of hemp rope to bind her already restricted body. Plus, of course, there were the sensory deprivation items—gag, blindfold, and earplugs, all made from the finest kid leather and designed to enhance Jennifer's experience. The last three items had been highly recommended by Samantha, who got so excited as she helped Jennifer dress that she suggested to Peter that they, too, should celebrate her rescue with some fun of their own.

Once inside the carriage, a highly enthused Jennifer watched as Shane studied the typed instructions for her upcoming bondage, instructions customarily given to the family butlers to apply to the patients before their stay at Peter's institute.

He looked impressed. "This is very clever. You will be totally restrained, my love, but without discomfort."

However, unbeknown to Shane, the dressing into her uniform and the viewing of her tailored state, together with the ritualistic methodology had driven Jennifer into a sensual frenzy. And when Shane began to apply the rope to her body by pulling her arms behind, it became all too much.

Shane appeared utterly bewildered as Jennifer turned sharply around, her vagina streaming, her mind and body aflame. She screamed at him. "I can't take this. I must have you now, my love, or I will go insane."

Clearly, Shane was on board with this suggestion, swiftly lifting Jennifer's skirt as she sat astride him. Then, after forever fumbling with his buttoned fly, he inserted his rock-hard penis into her extremely receptive sex, the open panties she wore affording Shane the easiest of entries.

There was no kissing, just screeching, animalistic sexual behaviour as she screamed her way to her first orgasm, the warm surge of Shane's own climax immediately following. Fortunately, he remained hard, as she quickly found her way to another and then another orgasm. *Fuck me. My first ever triple, amazing.*

She felt glorious, like an empress, as she sat astride her beloved, kissing his beautiful face, ecstatic that Shane was as sexually wild as ever. She had wondered if his cathartic experience might have tempered his sexual spirit, but fortunately, that was not the case.

"Oh, my darling, what a life we have in store."

Shane smiled, his not so rigid penis still inside her. "Fuck the life, Jen, what a *night* we have in store."

They both laughed, Shane assisting her as she lifted herself from his body before buttoning his fly. The ropes were in a sack, which he picked up. "You get yourself tidied up, I know how much you love that. Then I will bind you, nice and slow so that we can savour the moment. Then once I have you deprived of your senses, I will fuck you as *I* desire as we travel along. It's time the more sensible one of us took control."

Jennifer smiled as sensually as she could, responding appropriately to his ever so passionate suggestion. "Yes, my darling master. Your wish is my command."

Once on the other seat, Jennifer tidied herself up before settling into the luxurious leather. Suddenly she espied the fine, black instruments that would send her into a deaf, blind, and mute state on Shane's bench, to his right. Her mind and body instantly reacted, though this time in a more measured manner, her initial crazed state having been somewhat sated by her previous orgasms. As she savoured the thought of what was about to ensue, Shane came across and gently pulled her willing arms behind her, her mind and vagina alive with excitement.

"Are you ready my love?"

Ready? She couldn't wait. This had been her dream ever since she had met Shane and it was finally happening. She was dressed in tailored finery she never thought possible and was about to be taken, in every sense of the word, by her man, who loved her just as much, if not more than she loved him.

Rebecca was spending a pleasant evening in the company of Simone, Katerina, and Gigi. They had finished their light supper, and Simone and Katerina prepared to retire for the evening.

"I shall leave you in the care of Gigi, Rebecca. I am sure she will make you comfortable." Simone put her arm around her beloved Katerina and kissed her on the lips, all pretence of a non-sexual relationship thrown out the window in present company. They both said goodnight as they wandered upstairs, arm-in-arm, clearly in love.

Their attitude of accepting Rebecca into their fold was the reason she felt so relaxed. The three women from Victorian times had recognised her sapphic desires instantly. Just as contemporary Melbourne women, so inclined, also did. It seemed some things were universal, jumping not only geographical boundaries but also the boundaries of time.

She loved the elegant lifestyle of London society and the wide-eyed innocence of its participants, Phyllis and Georgina in particular. They were both such outgoing, positive women and she found it hard to believe that they once suffered greatly from their society's cursed, so-called, female *hysteria*. Since being exposed to their patriarchal culture, she now understood Peter's difficulties and his reasons for keeping his miracle cure of introducing these wonderful but sexually repressed ladies to their libidos, under wraps. Indeed, she now viewed him in the highest regard, his strange methods at the institute producing liberated, healthy ladies one after the other.

And speaking of sexual revelations, Rebecca sensed she was in for one of her own that evening. It was clear that Gigi was enamoured by her—why this was so continued to amaze her—but despite her best efforts, she remained an absolute simpleton in her presence.

They sat together on the sofa, Josephine having excused herself for the evening, both partaking of a port. Rebecca was still in her walking suit, her only set of clothes for what was meant to be a short stay. Gigi, on the other hand, had changed into an elegant evening gown bedecked with a diamond necklace that fell around her delicate neck as easily as a cascade fell over a rocky drop. *God, she is so pretty.* Rebecca longed to take her in her arms, but something was holding her back and she had no idea why.

"You are new to this aren't you?"

Rebecca shifted nervously on the couch. "Is it that obvious?"

Gigi was gazing into her eyes, causing Rebecca to avert her own eyes. She had never felt so vulnerable.

"You can touch me, I won't break," Gigi murmured.

And it was then that Rebecca realised what was holding her back. It was fear. Not of touching her, but of the fact that upon taking such liberty, her present world of romantic delight would crumble around her. She was in love with the fantasy of it all, a dream that would instantly vanish once captured by the harshness of reality.

Rebecca examined Gigi's beauty and grace with tears in her eyes, her heart and mind at a terrible impasse. And then it happened. Gigi leant across, desire gleaming in her eyes as she gently kissed Rebecca, keeping her gaze firmly fixed on Rebecca's as if she did not want her mind to escape. Rebecca closed her eyes as she felt Gigi's tender lips.

Gigi pulled back. "No, sweet lady. You shall not escape me. I want you to look at me when I kiss you."

Rebecca did as she was told, the two of them steadfastly staring at each other as their lips entwined. It was that moment, the combining of their bodies' forces while in fierce acknowledgement of the other, that showed Rebecca what it was to truly love another. Not incredibly, not fantastically, not dreamily, but truly. There was no stripping away of her dreams, no tumble from a higher plane, just a true, unembellished reality. It was as if Gigi had entered her thoughts, recognised them and had defeated them all in an instant. Never had Rebecca felt so empowered.

Without thought, she lifted her svelte lover into her arms and carried her up the stairs, all the while their eyes never once losing contact. She dropped her on the bed, all thoughts of tender moments thrown to the wind as she stood before her, both of them discarding their clothes as they kept their eyes locked on each other. *I know what she wants, this little bitch. And she is going to get it.*

Rebecca wanted, no *needed* to conquer her, to devour her, just as her willing victim also clearly desired. And as Gigi lie there displaying her God-given beauty, Rebecca gently eased down beside her, their eyes still locked as one.

She took control, breaking their eye contact as her tongue gently lashed Gigi's firm, pert breasts. Rebecca had no idea what was happening to her. It was as if her body had been taken over by another person, such was her desire. *Her breasts are so beautiful.* They had small areolas with protruding nipples and though small in size were superbly shaped. She tenderly kissed them before playfully nipping with her teeth, her lover reacting with erotic murmurings as her body writhed in delightful response. *Dear God, I am in heaven.*

As Rebecca's lips explored Gigi's bosom, her left hand slipped down to her vagina, her middle finger feeling how receptive her lover had become to her advances and how pronounced her clit was. The little love button that contained eight thousand sensitive nerve endings, twice the number of a man's penis. *Stiff shit guys.* Her middle and index fingers entered Gigi's moist vagina as initially they gently, then assertively imposed themselves on her privacy. And then, while forcefully holding her left nipple in her fingers, she ventured below, her dexterous organ tasting the sweetness of her lover's cum as it tenderly explored her vagina, searching for her magical spot.

She found it, Gigi reacting violently to her touch. Rebecca could sense her body arching, imagining her head pushing back against the pillow as she explored her sexuality, the taste of her lover sending Rebecca to even greater heights, inspiring her to amazing feats. Never had her tongue displayed such skill as she first kissed Gigi's clit, then gently caressing it, using only the tip of her tongue.

She felt Gigi's body tighten as she climaxed, her hands gripping the bed sheet, followed by a feverishly delightful groan, the sound of which was as music to Becky's ears, a symphony of glorious triumph. But she did not rest there, continuing to torture her lover in full realisation of the extreme sensitivity her clitoris was experiencing, softly licking her as she brought her down gently from her wondrous heights.

She moved up to her lover's side, locking her gaze with Gigi's once again, unable or unwilling to look away.

After a few tender moments, Gigi caressed Rebecca's cheek and smiled. "My turn now, my lovely." And with that, she moved down to Rebecca's exposed, receptive glory, Becky's mind alive with wonder as her body reacted to her beloved's tongue.

Rebecca was in a dilemma, which is why she had asked H G to come to Simone and Katerina's home that morning. The institute had a light schedule that day, only one four-hour treatment. Katerina was handling that while Simone was off somewhere with Gigi, taking her to inspect a venue that was for sale. It was Gigi's intention to set up a lesbian establishment in London, the main reason for her visit.

Consequently, she was alone with H G as they sat in the parlour.

"H G, I don't know what I am going to do?"

"Let me guess, you're in love with Gigi?"

At first, Rebecca was surprised, but then she smiled. "You're not guessing are you?"

"Not really, no."

"It's that bloody dowager again, isn't it? What has she got to say about me?"

"Well, the first thing she would be saying is if you intend to live in this society you will have to learn to curb your language."

Rebecca gasped. "Live here? How could I do that? I have a career at home that I worked extremely hard for. I have no intention of giving that up."

"There is no alternative. That is if you want to be with Miss Chevalier."

Miss Chevalier. The mere mention of her name created a tingle down Rebecca's spine, bringing forward images of her adorable minx. Gigi was the girl of her dreams who, just the evening prior had expressed her undying love for Rebecca, stating that she wanted them to be together forever.

Imagine that, a lifetime with Gigi. She would give anything for that. But would she? That was her dilemma. She came down from her cloud as the sound of H G's voice interrupted her daydream.

"Did you hear me, Rebecca, there is no alternative."

"Why not? She could come back with me."

"To your world of cars, planes, mobile phones, computers, and the internet? Don't be ridiculous. She would be isolated, utterly overwhelmed. Whereas you would be the exact opposite, not the slightest bit perturbed."

Christ, she is right. She could never allow that to happen, not to her lover, once again the mere thought of Gigi sending shivers up her spine. "But what about my career? I worked so hard to become an inspector."

"I think I could do something about that."

"You could? What?"

"Samantha's father is a good friend of the current police commissioner in London. He could inform him that you were responsible for rescuing his darling daughter from a fearful abduction, your consummate detecting skills saving her life. You would not be an inspector, but I am sure a post as a detective at Scotland Yard would be in the offing."

Could I really have a worthwhile career and a life with Gigi? It would be a dream come true. "Do you think it could happen?"

"Would you like to see the dowager's notes?"

"No, fuck the dowager. I am so over her."

"There is however a slight negative."

"And what is that?"

"The head of Scotland Yard is a renowned misogynist."

"So what's news?" She had been dealing with such arseholes in the police force all her working life.

"He will appoint you against his wishes, placing you in charge of an impossible cold case to prove his point."

"What case?"

"Jack the Ripper."

A blast of excitement hit Rebecca right between the eyes. *Jack the bloody Ripper? Imagine that, working on such a crime.* An idea immediately jumped into her head. "Do you think you could assist me?"

"Me? How could I do that?"

"Your bloody time machine. I understand there are several possible suspects. I could take the DNA of the Ripper from one of the victims and compare it to the DNA of the suspects, either eliminating them or convicting the killer."

"You want me to take you back to twenty-eighteen?"

"Yes, why not? You told me you could take me back to the time five minutes after we left so it would be seamless. I could pass the evidence to forensics for comparison without informing them what it was about." She was getting excited about the possibilities. "Picture it, solving the Ripper murders."

H G seemed to ponder over Rebecca's suggestion before responding. "I shall agree to your request, on one condition."

"And what's that?"

"That this will be the only case I shall assist you with. I cannot be spending DEMAT's precious energy jumping back and forth between time zones."

"Agreed. Besides, if I solve this case, I may become the head of Scotland Yard and get rid of that bloody chauvinist."

They both laughed. Rebecca was over the moon about her immediate prospects, while H G seemed particularly pleased with herself. *No doubt it's something between her fucking dowager and her.* But Rebecca could not give a rat's tail about that. She was going to be spending the rest of her days with her darling Gigi, and she couldn't wait to give her the news.

H G regained her attention. "I shall leave you to pass on your good tidings to Gigi, then I will join you after lunch. I have something I wish to discuss with you both. But first I need to speak with Samantha who has requested to see me on a most important matter."

CHAPTER ELEVEN

London 1898

Samantha was finally alone with H G in the dining room of the mansion after lunch. Peter was busy in his study screening applications for his institute, and Daria, who had stayed the night, was practising her karate. Something had been gnawing away at Samantha since her kidnapping, so she decided to come straight out and confront her friend. "H G, why did you dematerialise me?"

"So, you've worked that one out, have you?"

"It is obvious. I can understand that you didn't want me to have any knowledge of your machine so that I would pass Jenkins's polygraph test. But surely there is more to it than that?"

H G moved closer and sat next to Samantha, taking her hand. They were both in their walking suits at H G's request. Apparently, they had a small trip to make later that afternoon. Her expression was earnest, which troubled Samantha somewhat.

"First of all, it wasn't me who decided to dematerialise you — or should I say the Mark Two version of you. It was you."

"Me? Why on Earth would I do that?"

"Because you realised this era was not ready for the mathematical knowledge you gained about nuclear energy."

"Nuclear energy?"

"Yes. Humanity has learnt how to split the atom, its compounding effect creating a force capable of demolishing a city the size of London in an instant."

Samantha put her hands to her mouth. She was devastated. "Surely society has not deteriorated to such a state?"

H G smiled reassuringly. "It's all right, my darling. The two great atomic powers, the United States and Russia—"

Samantha interrupted her. "Russia? The Tsar agreed to such a thing?"

"The Tsar is no longer in charge. Russia becomes a Marxist state."

"Karl Marx? Russia has adopted the teachings of a German philosopher?"

"It's a long story, something we will no doubt discuss at length sometime in the future. But for the moment we should concentrate on what directly concerns us. Now as I was saying. So great is the power that these two nations possess, there is a real fear that a nuclear war could bring an end to the world. This horrifying thought has brought with it a period of unparalleled peace. There are smaller conflicts, continual struggles between capitalism and Marxism, but nothing on a worldwide scale."

How ironic. That it took such a monstrosity to bring about peace. "So it was me that decided to strip myself of such knowledge?"

"Indeed. You were adamant. Suggesting that there should only be one time traveller and that I was the best suited to the task."

Samantha thought about H G's last statement. *I think I know what is going on here.* "H G, you have us ready for a trip. Show me your time machine."

They both donned their gloves and bonnets and left the mansion, H G leading her into her residence, the outbuilding where Samantha had last seen their two-seater time machine. And there in its stead, stood the letterbox, the one from Jenkins's photos.

"Where did you come across such an idea?"

"From a television show."

"A what?"

"Never mind. We called it the DEMAT, short for dematerialisation. Let's go inside where you can see the true extent of your genius."

Samantha entered the DEMAT, the sheer size of its interior was astonishing. But far from being overawed, she was enchanted by it all. "I am responsible for this?"

"Exactly. It is a process called relativistic dimension. You took hold of Einstein's general relativity and went with it for days, weeks, one equation leading to another until you came up with this."

She followed H G to the central console where she showed her the controls. "The DEMAT is a space-time machine. This setting is for the time, this one for the location. It is very precise."

Samantha studied her great friend's expression as she explained how things worked. She could see how enthused, how involved H G was with her machine. And that was when she realised why she had asked for herself to be dematerialised. It wasn't, as she had told H G, purely because of the burden of her knowledge. It was because she could see how it would consume her, just as clearly as it was consuming H G. Which was fine for her, it was her life's dream — everything she had worked for and all she had ever wanted.

But the DEMAT wasn't that for Samantha. She was already living her dream with Peter, a dream that would one day bring her a family, children. *That* was why she had requested her own demise, as it were. She loved and valued her present existence so much and had seen, just as she now saw as she watched H G, how it would all change if she became a time traveller.

H G's smile was beaming. "Isn't it amazing, my darling?

137

Aren't we so clever? Where would you like to go? Africa? Australia? And what time? It's up to you."

Samantha slowly approached and embraced her good friend before smiling at her. She could feel the moisture in her own eyes as they stared at each other.

H G's eyes darted back and forth, searching hers, a confused look on her face. "What is it, Samantha? What is wrong?"

Samantha embraced H G again, squeezing her as hard as she could before releasing her and taking her hands in hers as they sat down. "I am so pleased for you, dearest friend. I can see how happy you are, how completed your life is."

"But aren't you happy too? Our dream has been realised."

"I am happy, as joyful as I have ever been. But not for me, darling, for you. I understand exactly how you are feeling at this moment. You have met your destiny, been reconciled with your fate. Just as I was the day Peter and I declared our love for each other. That was my kismet, this is yours. You want to take me on a journey? Well then lead me to the door and back to my life. That is where I belong, with my true love and with my work. My intense, fulfilling work. Nuclear energy is a destination H G, not a journey. And life is meant to be a journey, one to be cherished and savoured."

H G looked utterly bewildered. "So, are you saying that what I am doing is wrong?"

Samantha chuckled. "Good heavens, no. It could not be more right. For you. But only for you. This is an adventure that is yours and yours alone, to be savoured and enjoyed, but one that is not meant to be shared. Not with me, anyway."

H G looked down to where their hands were joined. "I may never find love."

"Are you looking for it?"

H G's gaze once again met Samantha's, then she shrugged

her shoulders. "Not really, no."

There was a moment's pause before they simultaneously burst into laughter, once again embracing each other as if it was the most natural thing in the world to do. Which, of course, for such true friends it was.

Samantha stood and took H G's hand. "Let's go, my darling."

"No, you go. I have an important journey to make."

"Of course, you have." Samantha smiled and left the DEMAT for what she imagined would be the first and last time.

H G thought about her conversation with Samantha as she set the DEMAT's coordinates for Simone and Katerina's residence. *God, I love Samantha. She is so wise and so damn clever.* She was extremely proud of her intelligent friend, without whom none of this adventure would have been possible.

But for the time being, as per the dowager's instructions, H G had an exciting proposition to put to Rebecca and Gigi. Everything was going exactly as planned, and what she was about to execute would put yet another of the major pieces of the puzzle into its rightful spot.

There were other important pieces to play out, one in particular, involving the murderous Simon that would change the whole course of events. But that was some way down the track.

Gigi and Simone returned home, taking off their gloves and bonnets before handing them to Josephine.

"Miss Rebecca is waiting for you in the parlour, Miss Gigi," Josephine informed her.

Simone kissed her on the cheek before excusing herself. "I

must see how Katerina is faring."

Gigi headed for the parlour, looking forward to seeing her new love, her heroine. She needed some cheering up. She and Simone had visited a bar in nearby Chelsea that was perfect for her plans, but it was a great deal more expensive than either of them had envisaged.

Of course, Simone had insisted that she and Katerina would sponsor it, but Gigi was having none of it. Fifteen thousand guineas was a small fortune, and she had no idea if what she had planned would succeed. She was prepared to risk her own life savings, a mere tenth of that amount, and would commit herself to a bank loan if she could get one, but she was unwilling to risk her friend's money.

Rebecca rose from the sofa and smiled at her as she entered the parlour. They embraced and kissed each other lovingly as if it was the most natural thing in the world. *It is so good to be in her arms again.* All the worries of the world had drifted away in an instant.

Rebecca continued to smile, looking exceedingly pleased with herself as they stood there, gazing into each other's eyes. "How was your day, my darling?"

"It was fine. But yours seems as if it was better. What's going on?" She was curious as to what would put such an expression on her lover's face.

"I have some amazing news. I am about to be appointed to New Scotland Yard as a detective."

Gigi's heart started beating rapidly. "Does this mean . . ."

"Yes, I can stay here in London and live with you."

Gigi could not believe her fortune. Tears tumbled from her eyes as she kissed and embraced her beloved. Suddenly, an idea flashed across her mind. "Perhaps we can have a commitment ceremony performed by Pastor Miller, just as Simone and Katerina experienced."

"A commitment ceremony? In Victorian London? Same-sex marriage has only just been legalised in Australia, and that's more than a century away."

Gigi gawped, bewildered by Rebecca's comments. "What on Earth are you talking about? I know Australia is an enlightened place but same-sex marriage? And what is all this talk of something being a century away."

Rebecca reddened, but then she smiled. "Oh, don't worry about me." She lifted Gigi off her feet, holding her in her powerful arms as she looked up at her with adoring eyes. "I am so in love I am in a muddled state, incapable of making any sense at all."

Gigi slowly slid down Rebecca's body into her loving embrace, and once again they shared a tender kiss.

Then Josephine entered the room interrupting the moment. "Miss Hope Grace Wells, ladies."

H G removed her bonnet and gloves before sitting opposite Rebecca and Gigi, who sat together, hand in hand, on the two-seater. It was clear to her that Gigi was elated with Rebecca's news and that they were deeply in love, which was imperative if the next step in her dowager's plan was to take place.

"So what is it that you have to discuss with us, H G?" Rebecca asked.

"It concerns Gigi's upcoming commercial venture."

Gigi turned to Rebecca in astonishment. "How could she possibly know about that?"

Rebecca smiled, patting Gigi's hand. "She knows everything about everything. She is some sort of seer."

Gigi's attention snapped back with an expression of reverence.

H G held up the large brown envelope she carried. "This money is the remainder of the recompense given to me by an anonymous donor. It has been used to sponsor George Best's journey to Melbourne as well as a dowry for yesterday's newlyweds. This leaves me with twenty thousand guineas which I was holding back until I was sure of a certain couple's commitment to each other."

She watched the reaction of Rebecca and Gigi who were staring at each other. Gigi's hands went to her mouth as she looked at her beloved in disbelief, then tears started streaming from her eyes as her face crumpled with emotion.

Rebecca's strong demeanour was instantly demolished as she took Gigi into her arms, joining Gigi with her own tears of joy. "I have no idea why you are so happy, my darling, but I am loving every moment of it."

"Don't you see? All my prayers have been answered. You're staying in London, and I am able to open my bar." Gigi turned to her while still embracing Rebecca. "Can this be truly happening?"

"I can assure you it is." H G handed Gigi the envelope. "Good luck with your enterprise Gigi. However, luck will have nothing to do with it. Your charming personality and your love of bohemian culture will establish Chelsea as a centre for your sapphic community . . . and a love nest for the two of you. Congratulations."

Gigi rose, coming over to embrace her before kissing her gratefully on both cheeks.

She accepted her affection with a smile.

Gigi sat beside Rebecca once again with her hands in her lap, clutching the envelope as though her life depended on it, which in fact it did. She looked into Rebecca's eyes. "My being at this moment is as happy as it has ever been. In the space of twenty-four amazing hours, my life has been transformed from one of hope to one of an exciting, breathtaking adventure." She looked up toward the ceiling. "Thank you, dear Lord, you will not regret this."

Melbourne 2018

Rebecca sat with H G in the forensic examiner's office, H G resplendent in her Victorian suit, hat, and gloves. Rebecca had explained H G's appearance by saying that she was a good friend and a character actor who was getting into her part, both in costume and by accompanying Rebecca as a policewoman.

They had appeared two days prior, seamlessly as Rebecca had predicted, with samples to be analysed, then returned at the appointed time for the DNA results, a matter of mere moments for them. H G had been careful to return them to a time after their original journey ensuring there would be no dematerialisation issues.

Her friend James, the chief examiner, had pushed the results through and soon Rebecca would see if the DNA of any of the nineteenth-century suspects matched that of the killer. *This is amazing, I am about to discover the identity of Jack the bloody Ripper.* But even more importantly she would put the arsehole in charge of Scotland Yard back in his place. Major General Stratford was a pompous man, who viewed women in the police force as a grave error, and as a means of proving his point had appointed Rebecca to reopen the Ripper file which had been officially closed in 1892.

"So what's the verdict, James?"

"There is no match between any of the specimens you gave me."

Shit, that's a surprise. She went to rise, but James continued.

"So we ran them through our database."

Rebecca shook her head. *Well, that was a nice waste of time, none of the specimens came from the twenty-first century.*

"And we found a match."

What? That is impossible. She turned to H G who smiled back at her, innocently.

"Are you certain? Which specimen?"

"The first one."

That was the Ripper's. "And who is it?"

"A Simon Lewis. He's in prison serving a life sentence."

What! She glared at H G who merely raised her eyebrows and continued to smile. *She knows exactly what's going on, the little bitch.*

She turned her attention back to James. "I know who Simon Lewis is. I put him there."

"So what is this all about? I've kept it off the books as you requested."

"Oh, it's nothing important, just a cold case." *Nothing important? Simon bloody Lewis is Jack the Ripper.* She wanted to throttle H G. "Thanks for your time, James. I appreciate it."

"What are you going to do with Lewis?"

"He's going to pay, don't you worry about that."

Tension rose as they left the examiner's office. Once inside the DEMAT, H G heaved a sigh of relief. She knew Rebecca was fuming and waited silently for the explosion.

"So, H G, what in the fuck is going on here? It's that fucking dowager, isn't it? Is this why you gave that sicko the knives and taught him how to use your machine. Well that turned out well, didn't it?"

"Are you suggesting that the story of Jack the Ripper should have been wiped from history? I am afraid he is far too important for that to happen. The extensive investigation into his crime alone advanced forensic science no end."

Rebecca frowned. "This destiny bullshit, it's all above my pay grade."

H G smiled at Rebecca's choice of words. *Above my pay grade? I like that, very pithy. Perhaps there is some hope for the future of the English language after all.*

"Well he's going to pay for it, mark my words," Rebecca grumbled.

"Indeed, he shall. What would you say to us taking him back to twenty-eighteen to serve out his life sentence?"

"Is that at all possible?"

"Indeed it is."

"Where is the bastard at the moment?"

"*At the moment?* Clearly, you have not grasped the concept of time as a fabric of the universe, have you?"

"I'm not the slightest bit interested in your mumbo jumbo, H G. Can you take me to him so I can arrest the psycho and put him where he belongs?"

"I can, and I will. At the moment in the space and time where we will be meeting Simon the Lewis, he is in dire need of our services. But once we have him in our grasp, you will have to become interested, in fact, become au fait with my *mumbo jumbo* if we are to deliver him to justice. Remember, if we send him back to prison at a time when he is already there, this second Simon will be dematerialised. Therefore, his crimes as Jack the Ripper will be expunged from his memory as only the first Simon will exist, and that Simon has no memory of his existence as the Ripper. Thus, it will be as if he is unpunished."

Rebecca rubbed her chin with a faraway look in her eyes, then she smiled. "Even better." She pointed her two index fingers at H G. "We will tell Simon Mark Two that he will be dematerialised. That will devastate him. Losing the memory of his greatest triumph? A lifetime punishment if ever there was one."

H G examined the smiling Rebecca. "It seems that you are more versed in time travel than either of us imagined."

She was about to set the coordinates to retrieve Simon when Rebecca grabbed her hand.

"There is a flaw in all this, isn't there?"

"Whatever do you mean?" She pulled the notebook from her pocket, turning the pages rapidly as she searched for the relevant page.

"He won't be in there for life, will he? Soon he will be going on his journey with us and become Jack the Ripper again."

It never failed to send a shiver up H G's spine when she read words that had just been spoken. She showed the passage to Rebecca that quoted her last sentence verbatim.

Rebecca responded with her usual vulgarity. "Fuck me. This is really weird shit."

It still troubled H G to hear the future ladies curse like drunken sailors, but she viewed it as a small price to pay for gender equality.

"Back to your concern. The situation can be as you so described Rebecca. But the good news is that it will always be the first Simon that accompanies us. So he will continually experience his heartache."

"What do you mean by *the situation can be*? I thought it was all predestined?"

"He has fulfilled his past destinies, becoming the unsolvable Jack the Ripper and changing the tide of the Scottish war of independence. But because part of his destiny is to return to twenty-eighteen, there is no need for him to time travel again, whereas all the others must, to ensure their destinies. The choice is yours. Keep him as the ignorant Simon, leaving him behind, or bring him with us and create Simon Mark Two, causing him to once again feel the pain of losing the memory of his triumph."

Once again Rebecca appeared bewildered, but then she smiled. "Now, let me see. Leave the first Simon in jail, in ignorant bliss, or bring him along, so once more he can feel completely miserable. I think we'll go with number two." Clearly, she was being sarcastic.

"Are you absolutely sure?"

"It's a no-brainer. Fuck him."

Okay then. H G looked up the coordinates in the dowager's instructions and set the dials accordingly, but before she could press the lever down Rebecca interrupted again.

"So what you are saying is that Samantha had to be kidnapped for all of this to happen. But you are the one responsible for it, sending the camera to Jenkins in the first place. Why don't we all just go back and do what we have to do without the drama?"

"There are several reasons. First of all, we had to ensure that Jennifer's ancestor George got involved and that he was directed to Australia rather than America, the reward money from Jenkins sponsoring him and allowing him to meet his future wife, Jennifer's great-great-grandmother. Then there is the financial backing of Shane and Jennifer, their involvement, along with Daria's, apparently the most important of all according to the dowager. And last, but not least, there is you and Gigi. Her bar becomes the genesis of the future LBGT, bohemian culture of Chelsea, while your appointment to Scotland Yard marks an important advance for female policewomen and London policing in general. And then there is your discovery of Simon as Jack the Ripper. Thus explaining why he never got caught. Except by us, of course, for which he is to be severely punished as you have just decreed. Satisfied?"

Rebecca nodded, but H G knew her companion still had one more question. She had seen the query written in the notebook.

"What would your very best friend Samantha say if she knew it was you that caused her to be abducted?"

"I would imagine a smart girl like Samantha, whose IQ would surpass yours and mine combined, has already worked that out. But being the true friend she is, her love is unconditional. This power of absolute love is the most potent force on the planet, as you are about to discover with your Gigi."

Rebecca smiled. "I think you're right. Okay, let's go and get this bastard. Where is he? And what is he up to?"

"He is in fourteenth-century Scotland, about to be hung by Robert the Bruce."

"What the fuck?"

It was comforting to know that some things never change. Rebecca's language as ribald as ever.

Chapter Twelve

Scotland 1314

Simon looked up at the noose as he stood at the steps of the scaffold. He wasn't sure how other people had reacted the moments before their execution, but all he could think of was how the rough rope would feel around his neck as he fell to his death. Not in a morbid sense, more in a technical, scientific sense. *I am a strange bastard, that's for sure.*

He didn't blame the Scots for what they were about to do to him, even though he had turned the war for them by introducing his guerrilla tactics. It was the ensuing peace that had proven his downfall, just as it had back in 2018. *Back? How fucked up is that? This time-travel shit is crazy.*

Peacetime was not a good place for a murderous soul like him. Simon was far more at peace when he was cutting people's flesh, and his darkness flourished in a wartime environment. But once order and harmony became the norm, he was lost. Eventually, the disquiet within had taken over, and he soon found himself cutting innocent peoples' throats whenever the opportunity arose. Male or female, young or old, it mattered little to Simon because it was not a sexual thing for him, just a cancerous need that he had been blessed with from birth.

As he stood there, the noose around his neck and the crowd cheering for his demise, he felt nothing. He always knew he would come to a violent end and he was grateful it was all about to finish He watched as the executioner walked across to the lever, soon to dispatch him to Hades when, all of a sudden, he heard the familiar, whirring noise. *Fuck me, it's H G and the DEMAT.*

The crowd moved back, astonished as the DEMAT materialised before their eyes. They were clearly overawed by the phenomenon, only Robert the Bruce stood there unafraid. His hands were on his hips as the wind pushed against his thick locks.

The assembly let out a collective gasp as two women stepped out of the cylindrical box. It was H G . . . and Rebecca. *That fucking bitch.* He had no idea why she was there, too, but he knew it did not bode well for him.

King Robert approached and embraced H G. "You are back." He turned and looked up at Simon. "You did well for us great seer, but as you can see your warrior is of no further use to us. His barbaric soul not suited to our time of peace and joy."

H G nodded to Robert the Bruce, then stepped back, throwing her arms into the air, speaking loudly so all could hear her. "I am back to take our fallen God from you."

The people were obviously in awe of the diminutive woman as she stood there in her bonnet and gloves, her arms outstretched to the sky.

Even Robert the Bruce seemed taken aback. "Fallen God you say? I had no idea he was thus blessed."

She continued to shout her words as if speaking to the Gods in the sky, which Simon found curious as only Robert and a few others understood what she was saying.

"Blessed you say? He is far from blessed, good sir. We are about to place him into an eternal hell from which he can never escape, unlike your temporary death, whereupon he would come at you all as a spectre, a shadow of the night, and rain upon your village a terror never before seen. You can hang his mortal soul, Robert the Bruce, but in so doing you will release a phantom."

King Robert had fear in his eyes as he looked at the hangman, giving him instructions in Scottish that Simon, after four years of living amongst them, understood. "Cut the devil loose but keep him bound and bring him to H G, the mighty seer."

He turned to H G. "You are welcome to him. I have never met such a barbaric soul. He belongs in hell if ever a man did."

Rebecca grabbed Simon by the arm and pulled him to the DEMAT. H G put her arms down and then slapped Robert the Bruce's huge upper arm. "You are a mighty warrior, King Robert, and it has been a pleasure to know you."

King Robert responded in kind, very nearly knocking H G off her feet. "And you, wondrous seer, have assisted us greatly. God speed, and travel in peace."

With that, H G led the way into the DEMAT, sealing the door behind them. She went across to the console, setting her new coordinates. Her attention turned to him, and he merely smirked at her cunning.

"Time to get you cleaned up and into your prison uniform, Simon. You're going back where you belong."

Simon frowned, realising what she possibly meant. "When you say back, what do you mean? After Shane and I left the prison, or before?"

Rebecca smiled at him in a very unfriendly way. "Before, dick-shit. My choice."

H G intervened. "Saturday, the day before we left. The laundry will be unoccupied so your return will be unnoticed."

"But my other self will be there. I will be dematerialised you bitches."

Rebecca smiled, clearly enjoying herself. "Now, now, flattery will get you nowhere, Simon the Lewis, or whatever you are calling yourself nowadays. Let's see, in the twenty-first century it's plain old Simon Lewis, but what was it in the nineteenth century?"

"Fuck you."

"That's right. You were called Jack, Jack the Ripper.'

"That's right, you cunt, and I am so looking forward to slitting your throat," Simon scoffed.

Rebecca pulled her revolver from her jacket, holding it with two hands as she pushed it against his temple.

He smiled. "Go ahead, you bitch. You would be doing me a favour. I know what you two have got planned for me, a permanent loop where I go from being an ignorant inmate to become Jack the Ripper and then back to my former unaware self."

"Don't fall for it, Bec, he wants to live, trust me," H G said. "You will get what you want, his eternal punishment. Get him cleaned up but keep him handcuffed throughout. I will park us somewhere quiet while you do that, then we will return to the prison laundry as planned."

She's right. I do want to live and for a good reason. Saturday? A plan was formulating in his brain. He knew two things that neither of them knew. He knew exactly where he, the other Simon, would be at a certain time on a Saturday and that he, they, had a twin brother who was in Bali somewhere. A situation he could use to his advantage. All was far from lost. His evil mind was working overtime as he willingly let himself be cleaned up and dressed for his return.

Melbourne 2018

Simon Mark Two was clean-shaven again and wearing his prison uniform. He had been deposited in the laundry by H G and that bitch Rebecca, left to his own devices to avoid being dematerialised.

He recalled Rebecca's remarks from the door of the DEMAT after they had left him on the laundry floor. "Good luck with your efforts of avoiding your former self, pea brain. You'll have to exist like the Phantom of the Opera." She had roared with laughter, H G looking at him knowingly as she closed the door.

Fucking cunt, Rebecca. I will slash her throat one day. But for now, Rebecca didn't concern him. It was H G's attitude and her actions that were making him feel uneasy. Why hadn't she made *certain* that he would be dematerialised by Simon Mark One? It was not like her to leave things to chance. Plus, she was always banging on about how everything was predestined. *Well, maybe this time she's fucked up?* Neither she or Rebecca, or her smart-arse dowager knew anything about his twin brother in Bali, or wherever the fuck he was now. And that was the fly in the ointment he would use to his advantage. Plus, he knew exactly where Simon Mark One would be on a Saturday.

He looked at the clock on the laundry wall. One o'clock, perfect. It was as if everything was falling into place.

Simon Mark One went to the library as he always did at two o'clock on a Saturday. Because it was a Saturday the place was deserted, all the sports nuts gathered around the televisions in the rec room watching the AFL or the cricket or whatever the fuck the dickheads watched.

He walked up to the prisoner in charge at the counter. "Simon Lewis to collect my usual book."

The guy looked up, surprised. "You've already picked it up."

Simon was as shocked as someone as pathological as him could be, raising one eyebrow. "What are you talking about?" He stared at the duty prisoner, his cold glare having the desired effect.

The hapless inmate was clearly shitting himself as he replied nervously. "You made a point of saying you would be at your normal table."

What the fuck? He turned and headed for the table in question, the one in the far corner where he would regularly read his favourite book, *The Definitive History of Jack the Ripper,* in seclusion.

And there it was, the large volume sitting on the desk waiting for him.

He sat at the table and opened the book at the beginning, and there was a hand-written note, in his own hand. *Fuck me, what's going on here?*

He read the note.

Simon, this is you, me, us writing this note. Look up at the end of the aisle, and you will see me, you.

He looked up, and for the first time in his, life his heart skipped a beat. It was him, smiling and waving back at him. *Jesus Christ.*

The other version of him spoke in a whisper, just loud enough for him to hear. "I know this is freaky but I, you, we, have just come back from eighteen-ninety-eight where we fulfilled our destiny."

Despite the unreality of the situation, Simon found himself unperturbed. "Go on."

The other Simon was taken aback somewhat, but then he smiled. "Of course, I forgot what I was like back then. You, we, always sensed we were meant for greater things, didn't we?"

Simon was by now intrigued, and as a consequence, slightly impatient. "All right, get on with it. What's this all about? It's not like me to beat around the bush." He started to rise to approach his counterpart.

"No, don't move." The other him looked intense, his eyes aflame, his hands outstretched. "If you come within five metres of me, I will dematerialise."

"You'll what?" Simon sat back down.

"Dematerialise, disappear in a puff of smoke if you like."

Simon was rapt. "So if I walked over there I could kill myself?"

"No don't." He looked alarmed. "I know how much fun that would be for you, but it is in your best interests to keep me alive."

Simon stood up, smiling as he moved and sat on the edge of the table, a metre closer to himself. He was thoroughly enjoying himself. "Oh yes, and why is that?"

"I can get you your freedom. I've got a plan."

"It better be a good one. I'm becoming a bit excited about the idea of seeing myself go up in a puff of smoke."

The other Simon looked extremely unnerved. "Fuck, I forgot what a homicidal maniac I am. Listen, it's simple. I will stay here in the library while you get Shane to come here and knock me out. That way I will be sent to the infirmary, away from you."

Simon stood up. "I'm still not seeing it. Get to your point."

His other self put his palms up. "I will. I will. It's brilliant, trust me."

Simon laughed. "Trust myself? You must be kidding me?"

"Poorly put, you're right. Hear me out. It's about our twin brother, Bridge."

Simon winced at the sound of Bridge's name. "That treacherous prick. He's the reason Shane and I are in here."

"Exactly. But we can use him to get you out of here. Then once you are free, you can collect Shane's stash. Do you remember where it is?"

"Do you?" *Fucking idiot, if he does, then I do.*

"Fair enough. Anyhow, once you've got the money, you'll

have the ways and means to track the bastard down and cut his throat if you like."

Simon sat down, the thought of killing his twin brother appealing to him. "So what's your plan?"

"When I am in the infirmary, you will go to the guards and tell them you need to speak to the Police Minister Susan Turnbull. As you know, she knows about Bridge."

"Why would she bother? She has us in prison."

"As soon as she hears the mention of the name Bridge Lewis, she will shit herself. Remember she is in this right up to her neck. She let Bridge and the others escape."

Simon liked it. "She will. You're right. So then what happens?"

"You tell her that you are Bridge. And that I, Simon, organised to have you, Bridge, kidnapped so that I would have you, Bridge, take my place in this shit hole. But you, Bridge, knocked me, Simon, on the head and escaped."

Simon thought about this for a moment, the other Simon interrupting his thoughts.

"I know what you are thinking about."

Of course, he fucking does. "Oh yeah, and what is that?"

"How will she be able to tell that you're Bridge and not Simon?"

Fuck he's right. That is what I'm thinking about. "Okay genius. Remember you've been thinking about this longer than me."

"It's not a pissing contest, Simon. We're on the same team here, literally."

Simon was getting sick of this prick. The guy was beginning to sound like a whining brother. He stood. "Don't forget who's in charge here, dip shit."

"Listen to yourself. You are calling yourself names. I am you, mate. Now, I know that means jack shit to you at this present moment, but think about the end prize, your freedom. You'll have the ability to revenge us both and to slice a few more throats along the way. Trust me you'll enjoy that."

"You seem to be partial to throat-cutting all of a sudden. Anyhow, answer our question. How will I convince Turnbull that I am Bridge?"

"That's easy. You will bring her to the infirmary and I, Simon, lying in bed, will confess that I did it."

Simon thought about this. "How will she know that you are Simon and not Bridge?"

"Think about it. If it was Bridge lying there, he would hardly be confessing to being Simon, would he?"

Fuck, he's right. Shit, I'm getting smarter in my old age.

"Okay, I agree. So what do you want me to do?"

"Go to Shane and tell him to come here and knock me out. Then contact Minister Turnbull. You should be out and free by the end of the day so you can get our revenge on our twin brother. You can slit Turnbull's throat too if you like, I know I would."

This statement prompted another thought to flash through Simon's mind. "How come you don't want to be free? You just said you would like to slit her throat."

"Because I have unfinished business back there, and, because I have prior knowledge, I will be able to manipulate the situation to my, our, advantage. They fucked up this time. They didn't know that I would know exactly where to meet you or that we have a twin brother. This H G bitch follows her dowager's instructions slavishly, which means she's finally fucked up."

"Hold on, you say to our advantage? How is it to mine?"

"Because I am going to go back and cut Rebecca Browning's throat, how does that sound?"

That fucking bitch. He knows how much I hate her and would love to slice her throat. But this bastard knows the terrain. "So when will you be going back?"

"Shane and I will leave tomorrow."

"Shane and you?"

"Yes, but they will think it's you, not me. That's what's going to fuck them up."

Susan Turnbull had found it hard to believe what she had heard. Bridge Lewis back in Melbourne? But even more unbelievable was the fact that he was in prison and needed to speak to her personally. She had no idea what it was about, but she knew she had to meet with him. He had far too much knowledge on her involvement in his and his accomplices' getaway to Bali last year.

She entered the room and there he was. He looked desperate as he stood up to greet her. His hands were cuffed in front of him, a burly prison guard at the ready.

"Susan, thank Christ you are here."

She turned to the guard. "Leave us alone."

After the guard left the room, she turned to Bridge. She knew she could speak openly as the room was used by lawyers and their clients, so it was private. "What in the fuck is going on here, Bridge? If that is who you actually are. She couldn't tell. He still had the same evil, green eyes as his murderous twin brother.

"Oh, it's Bridge, you will see that when you visit Simon in the infirmary."

"Infirmary? What in the fuck is wrong with him?"

"I bopped him on the head, just as he was about to do to me. Then he was going to make out like he was me and call you to verify it."

"Just as you could be doing right now. All right, let's go down to infirmary. I know there are only two of you, so one of you has to be Bridge."

They headed down to the infirmary with the guard accompanying them. Just as Susan opened the door, Bridge stepped back. "What's wrong with you?"

"I don't want to go in the room. I am still shit frightened of him. You know what he is like."

Susan studied his face, and he did appear terrified. *That makes sense.* "You stay here, I don't need you. This bastard will tell me everything I need to know." She turned to the guard. "Keep an eye on him, I'll be back shortly."

She entered the room and there was the green-eyed monster, sitting up in bed, a bandage around his head, his hands strapped to the bed. He smiled at her in his menacing way and instantly she knew who it was.

"Hello, Minister, so good to see you."

"What made you think you could get away with it, Lewis? You two are about as alike as chalk and cheese."

He chuckled. "Is that right? You always were the clever one, weren't you? A bit like that Browning bitch. I heard you made that carpet muncher an inspector. What did she have to do to earn that, I wonder?"

"Put bastards like you where they belong." Clearly, he was not trying to hide his true identity and she wondered why. "You have given up your pretence?"

He smiled as he leant back against the pillow. Even in his subordinate position, his menace was ever-present. *This bastard is pure evil.*

"What can I say? My twin got the jump on me, caught me off guard. I should have known, he's me after all, isn't he?"

"Just because he's your twin, he's far from being you. He's outside this room now, shit frightened to face you."

He huffed. "So that's what he told you? Very clever. Anyhow, you tell him I am sorry, I had to do it. I hope he has no hard feelings."

She had had enough of talking to this prick. "Goodbye, Simon. I hope I never see your evil face again."

He started laughing, his laughter without humour—wicked, malicious. "I wouldn't bet on that, Ms Turnbull. I reckon you'll be seeing me sooner than you could ever imagine."

She looked at him as if he were mad, which of course he was. "Goodbye, Simon. Enjoy your life's journey." And with that she turned and walked away from him, hearing his rant as she left the room.

"I will, you silly bitch, I will."

Even though Susan was never in danger, she was relieved to be leaving Simon's poisonous presence. *Imagine being at that prick's mercy.* She turned to the guard, nodding her head toward Bridge. "Take off his cuffs, he's coming with me."

Susan sat in the driver's seat of her car with Bridge sitting beside her. She had dismissed her driver for the next few days so she could be alone with Bridge and was looking forward to talking to him to find out how Orisa and Tori were faring in their new lives in Bali—or wherever they were—a fact she neither needed nor wanted to know. She had grown to like the tall African, Orisa, and her submissive partner, despite the fact the former Nigerian princess was an accomplice, though somewhat unwilling, of Shane's.

"Let's get you into some new clothes. I suppose you'll need money to get back to wherever you came from. I'll fix all that up. You can stay with me tonight and leave tomorrow. Is that okay with you?"

Bridge smiled, and for a fleeting moment, she felt Simon's presence, dismissing it instantly as Bridge's true nature shone through. "Thank you so much, Susan. You are a life saver. I will never forget your kindness."

"You're welcome. We have so much to talk about. How are the two lovebirds, Orisa and Tori?"

"The last time I saw them they were as happy as ever."

Susan smiled, looking forward to having Bridge over for the night and catching up with the news. She pulled on to the freeway, headed for the city where she would buy Bridge some clothes and withdraw some cash for him before heading home where she would cook dinner. She loved cooking, especially preparing all the ingredients, her new set of steak knives making this task even more enjoyable.

CHAPTER THIRTEEN

London 1898

H G had to collect Daria at the Rhodes mansion before travelling to the institute to meet with Jennifer and Shane. Daria looked as bright and as positive as ever in her bonnet and gloves, her dark hair up in a fashionable chignon, her slim athletic figure accentuated by her dark suit.

"All set, Daria?"

Her grin went from ear to ear. "Absolutely. What an adventure, back to eighteen-eighty-five with the newlyweds. And me with the most important task of all according to the dowager."

H G could tell that this fact was extremely important to this bravest of people. Jennifer had told her about Daria's past. How she had spent many years as a personal slave to a cruel tyrant, and how she had overcome this trauma to surface as a fighting warrior, ready to defend Jennifer with her life. "Would you like me to tell you what the dowager said about you?"

Daria's face came alive with interest and excitement. "Yes please."

H G turned to the relevant page in the notebook and shared the passage. *Daria is the bravest and most loyal person one could ever want as a friend and protector. She must be informed of the importance of her mission as she accompanies her great friend and her new husband on their journey. The whole success of the mission depends on her.*

H G looked up to see the slim, beautiful warrior's eyes filled with moisture, clearly proud of who she was and of her importance to the project.

H G put her arm around Daria's shoulders. "We all so love and admire you, Daria. For you to overcome what happened to you and come out of it as such an accomplished person has been a remarkable achievement."

Daria stood up straight and proud, even with tears tumbling from her eyes. H G said nothing else as she turned to the console and set the coordinates for the institute.

Jennifer and Shane had spent the most spirited, yet delightful, first day and evening together as husband and wife. After their initial impromptu lovemaking, they had gone back to script, Shane tying her in her uniform and depriving her of her sight, sound and hearing with the soft, leather instruments as they rode along in the carriage.

The ride seemed forever to Jennifer as she experienced her lover's manhood no less than five times, the first of these sitting astride of him, the final time lying on the floor of the carriage as once again she felt the warmth of his passion erupt into her ever willing body.

Even though her arms had been tied behind her and trussed to her corseted body for the two-hour journey, Peter's binding instructions were so precise and skilful that her arms had maintained their feeling throughout.

And such was the enthusiasm of Shane's passion it had given them ample time to have Jennifer untied and able to spend the last ten minutes of the journey in her husband's loving arms, sitting on his lap as they looked at each other like lovesick schoolchildren.

The institute was as beautifully appointed as Peter had mentioned, and they had been given use of the master guest suite. Although they were probably the kinkiest couple in Victorian London, their first evening in bed together as man and wife was as vanilla as could be. Though they did make love in their Victorian nightgowns, just for the heck of it, adding some measure of spice to their intimacy.

Consequently, when Daria and H G arrived the next morning, she and Shane were fully sated in all senses of the word. Jennifer wore a normal walking suit, her uniform packed away in the single suitcase she was taking on their journey.

H G had requested time with her alone, so they had wandered off into the magnificent gardens of the institute.

Once they were alone, H G's expression became extremely serious. "Jennifer, what I am about to say to you is of the utmost importance." She then handed Jennifer an envelope. "Inside is a list of the quotes taken from the dowager's notebook, which I typed out for you last night. The dowager instructed me to give them to you in preparation for the novel you intend to write once you arrive at your destination. I have also typed the complete details of our journey. Details you were not privy to. She stressed that this information would prove vital to your task."

Jennifer took the envelope, not overly concerned about it. All she could think of at that moment was the memory of her husband's manhood entering her time after time the night before. Indeed, her mind was more on their next romantic adventure, rather than H G and her dowager's future plans.

H G continued. "Shane has his book on shares and property movements, so he should turn your twenty-five thousand guineas into a fortune."

She then leant over and embraced her. "So, until next we meet, my friend."

Jennifer was surprised by this show of sentiment. H G

had always presented herself as the ultimate professional, but she gratefully accepted it. She and Shane, along with Daria, were going to a place and time foreign to them. That thought bringing her mind away from her beloved for the briefest of moments and prompting a question. "H G, I know we are travelling back to eighteen-eighty-five, but where is our new location?"

"In London. I have travelled back there and arranged for your rented lodgings, a spacious, fully furnished residence opposite Hyde Park."

Jennifer smiled, although her thoughts returned to Shane. *He is so clever, my wonderful man.* It was then she realised that she had been off the pill since arriving in Victorian London, and instantly thoughts of little children running around their new residence flashed through her romantically inclined mind.

She turned to H G. "Will we have a family?"

"It is not mentioned by the dowager, but that doesn't surprise me as it is irrelevant to our ultimate task."

"And what is that task, H G?"

"I have no idea."

Jennifer gasped. "But surely it has a purpose?"

"Oh, it has a purpose, I am already aware of some of those predestined paths. But as to its overall aim, I am as ignorant as the rest of you. The one thing I am certain about is that, whatever her ultimate aim is, it is for all of our benefits."

She took Jennifer's hands, squeezing them as if to emphasise her point. "It is imperative you start your book as soon as we arrive, do you understand me?"

Her sudden seriousness startled Jennifer somewhat. "Don't worry, H G. I know how to structure a book. I will compile all of your quotes and detailed chronology of our adventure into note form on the day we arrive, and from there it is just a matter of constructing the novel with imaginative, interesting dialogue. Something I am extremely adept at, I can assure you."

This seemed to appease and relieve H G, the stress on her face at once relaxing. "Just promise me you will do it as soon as you get there. I sense your world is about to become very busy."

Is it now? Her expressed sentiment intrigued Jennifer. Perhaps she was right about babies arriving?

A tingling entered her mind and body as soon as she thought about the possibilities of her future, imagining the wonderful life that was in store for three of them. Her world had become complete, with a different, less egocentric purpose.

Despite her reverie, she vowed to herself that she would comply with H G's directions and compile her notes for her novel, which clearly was an important part of the dowager's plans. In fact, it may even be the ultimate prize at the end of their adventure—her book inspiring thousands of people, showing the world, especially young women, that all things were possible. Provided the spirit of adventure was there.

Jennifer was utterly taken aback when H G passed her a notebook. "H G, what's this?"

"Just a parting gift. I saw it in a book store and noticed how similar it was to the dowager's. So I thought it appropriate that I should purchase it for you."

"Similar? I reckon it's an exact copy, the gold trimmings, the exquisite binding. Where is the dowager's?"

"It's securely locked away in a safe in one of the rooms of the DEMAT. I only bring it out when necessary, such is its preciousness."

H G's solemn expression grabbed Jennifer's undivided attention. "I won't see you for quite a while. Not until this moment has once again passed in time. You, Shane, and

Daria must take particular care that you don't run into your former selves or else you will be dematerialised. Of course, once the time you leave for eighteen-eighty-five arrives — which is now — from that time onwards, you will be safe, as, naturally, none of you will be here in your present form."

Jennifer shook her head and chuckled. "God, H G, you're a marvel keeping track of all this."

"Yes, it does keep me fully occupied. But you won't have to worry about it too much. I will inform Shane and Daria of this requirement when we are in the DEMAT."

H G stood. "Time to go. You will find a complete set of new clothes expertly tailored for you all in the wardrobes of your new home." She smiled. "You will do well, Jennifer, as will Shane, and especially Daria. She has the most important part of all to play."

"Really?" Jennifer was both surprised and delighted. "Have you told Daria? She will be tickled pink."

"I have, and she is, believe me. Such a positive soul is your friend, Jennifer. You are lucky to have her."

Jennifer merely smiled. She well knew how fortunate she was to have her bestie by her side, something that would not have happened if not for the evildoing of Shane's former self.

London 1885

Jennifer mused over the accuracy of H G's, or rather the dowager's predictions. From the moment the trio had arrived, they had been flat out. Shane had their fortune to make, so he was fully employed, leaving early in the morning and returning home in the evening, sharing his time during the day between the stock exchange and real estate brokers. He had never been busier in his life and, as he expressed to her and Daria, had never been more happily occupied.

The large home, the furniture, and all of their clothes were superb, as H G had promised. Before she left, she had explained that such a household required extensive management, and in that era, this management was commonly carried out by several servants, including the most important of all, a housekeeper. After all, it wasn't as though there was a supermarket down the road. Therefore, all the food had to be bought from various traders who delivered it to the house. The maids had to be managed, and all the accounts for things such as the expenses of the household, bills of tradesmen, and other incidentals had to be kept, all duties normally managed by the housekeeper.

Jennifer and Daria had initially decided to share the housekeeper duties, but as she had to write her book, most of the organisation was left to Daria, who revelled in the responsibility. As there was only the three of them, only two maids were required, one for cleaning and one for cooking. However, all that changed when Jennifer became pregnant.

She had been elated at the discovery, and Daria was excited about becoming an *auntie*. Shane's reaction was animated, the news seeming to inspire him to greater heights. He threw himself more diligently into managing their funds armed with the knowledge of his book from the future, which never left his side.

Naturally, Jennifer was the most affected, and not just for the obvious reasons. When they had first arrived, she had devoted all of her energy and attention toward the book, spending countless hours on compiling the storyline, not only arranging it chronologically but inserting all the various quotations in the relevant places in the notebook H G had given her. The bulk of her writing was cursive, but she printed the quotes in block form, so they stood out.

But once she knew of her pregnancy, she had stopped her writing. The outline of the story, or the *donkey work* as she called it, had been completed. So she had put the notebook away in a drawer, vowing to come back to it after she had given birth, which in those times was an extremely danger-ous undertaking. Because of the dangers, Jennifer had dedi-cated herself entirely to the task of keeping herself in perfect health. The motherhood instinct absolutely dominated her psyche.

Daria had taken complete responsibility for the house-hold. Shane's continued success enabled her to hire several more servants, one employed explicitly as a lady's maid for Jennifer.

So by the time the baby arrived, a beautiful, blue-eyed blonde bombshell who they named Shelly after Jennifer's mother, theirs was a typical, late Victorian household run with military precision by Daria, who still maintained her karate exercises. This particular activity had caused much interest amongst the servants, Daria's discipline earning her the moniker of the *warrior housekeeper* amongst them.

With their extended family, they found their social lives similarly enlarged. Within a year they had moved to a man-sion that still adjoined Hyde Park but on a much better street—Park Lane. The Courtneys were quite the family in their neighbourhood. Their home often hosted dinner parties with the families of Shane's business colleagues. Daria's presence at the table justified by the explanation that she was Jennifer's cousin.

However, throughout their escapades, all three took spe-cial care to avoid any publicity, as well as making sure that they remained separate from their future friends. And not just those who were unaware of the time travel, which were Pastor Miller and Georgina, Simone and Katerina, and Derek and Phyllis Jones. For example, Peter and Samantha Rhodes would not know of the trios' existence until 1898, so they were also to be avoided at all costs.

Jennifer, at first, missed Rebecca terribly, but with the addition of another two children, Betsy and Graham, she found herself far too engaged with her duties to bother about anything other than her family and her household. She was so grateful to have Daria by her side, and she was sure she and Shane could not have managed without her. Clearly, this was what H G was referring to when she stressed the significance of Daria's involvement.

London 1897

H G had completed the last of the dowager's instructions and all the notations in the notebook except one. It was the last inscription, and it appeared to be very special because it was written in bold capitals.

DEMAT APPEARS FOR A BRIEF MOMENT THEN DISAPPEARS ON THE WESTERN SIDE OF PARK LANE ON THE 20th FEBRUARY 1897.

H G was puzzled by this. It was the first time the dowager had been generic rather than specific. There was no time given. And why did the DEMAT make such an appearance? There was no context to it, no events leading to it. It was as though it was an isolated event, completely unconnected to everything. She decided to go to the library and look up the newspapers around that date.

After an extensive search, she finally found a small article on page twenty of the London Times that sent a shockwave through her body.

Woman Killed Saving Friend. Yesterday on Park Lane, outside Hyde Park, a young lady by the name of Miss Daria White was trampled to death after throwing herself in front of a runaway steed, this heroic act saving her friend, a Mrs Jennifer Courtney and her three children.

H G was in tears, thinking of her beautiful friend while at the same time admiring her bravery. *This* was the importance of Daria's involvement that the dowager had so earnestly stressed. She had saved Jennifer's life. And this clearly was the reason why the DEMAT had to appear on that day and at that place.

But still, there was no time given. What was the dowager playing at? She decided to look in the obituaries. And there it was, an anonymous notice aside from the Courtney family's obit. *Daria White killed at three thirty precisely.*

She wondered about the complicated trail and the reasoning behind it. And then it came to her. There was no mention of the time in either the article or Shane and Jennifer's notice, simply because there was no reason to mention it by either of the parties. To the Courtney family, it was purely a heartfelt eulogy to a departed loved one, while the reporter in the Times was merely relaying the facts.

Clearly, the anonymous notice was from the dowager. And rather than give the time that it had happened in her notebook, she had made H G investigate so that she would be made aware of the tragedy, and of Daria's ultimate sacrifice. *How thoughtful and sweet of her.*

She returned to the Rhode's mansion and entered her residence and then the DEMAT. Never had she been so determined to get something right. After setting the precise coordinates, H G pushed the lever down, the DEMAT making its whirring sound as she arrived at her location. She turned on the exterior camera and there they were across the road, Daria with Jennifer and her three children.

Clearly, the familiar sound of the DEMAT had gained their attention as their heads turned and they all walked across to investigate its sudden appearance. And just then a giant, white, runaway horse went thundering by behind them. H G breathed a sigh of relief, then immediately reset the DEMAT's coordinates, heading back to her residence. She saw the shocked look on Jennifer and Daria's faces as she dematerialised before their eyes.

After arriving home from saving Daria and preventing Jennifer and her children from witnessing such a traumatic event, H G relaxed, and the gravity of the whole situation hit her like a ton of bricks. Her body was trembling, and she started crying uncontrollably, her arms wrapped around her body as she sat on the floor, rocking backward and forward.

Eventually, the shock of it all faded, and H G was able to stand and wipe her tears away. That was when she realised how alone she was in her adventures. There was no one to share her grief or her trauma. Her existence, the world of a time traveller, was a solitary and very lonely one, something that her wise friend Samantha had foreseen and had wanted no part of.

But for H G there was no alternative. This was her chosen path but even more than that, it was her destiny.

London 1897

Jennifer returned home with Daria and the children after witnessing the mystery of the DEMAT's sudden appearance and immediate disappearance. She had been so busy with her life that she had basically forgotten all about its existence. Was that the reason for its sudden appearance? Was it trying to send her a message?

She left the children with Daria and went to her study, taking out her notebook from the drawer of her desk, something she hadn't looked at or thought about for over a decade.

Jennifer opened the notebook, and that was when she noticed the date of the first entry, the day that H G had met the mystical dowager. It was the next day. A shiver ran up and down her body. Suddenly she realised who she was, and what she was meant to be doing. She was a writer, a story-teller, but she had taken her eye off the ball, something she would instantly fix. Hers was an important message. She immediately took a piece of paper, inserted it into the type-writer and started typing furiously, determined to relay that message to her audience.

Jennifer watched from her first-floor window as her visi-tor walked up the street, acknowledging a now bearded Shane and the children. Jennifer had excused herself from their usual Sunday walk after lunch, Daria also giving the servants the afternoon off, leaving the two of them alone in the house.

She had typed throughout the night, preparing her de-tailed synopsis, making sure that everything was included and listened as Daria, who was wearing a blonde wig, an-swered the door and welcomed her caller.

"Good afternoon. Madame is waiting for you in the par-lour."

She sat down in her chair, her typed work in an envelope with her notebook in her lap. Just before the door opened, she pulled the black veil down over her face.

The young lady entered the room. "Good afternoon, my name is H G Wells. I believe you sent for me."

EPILOGUE

Simon sat in the back of the police car, cuffed and ready to be taken back to prison. He had taken every precaution, not going to Shane's secret stash hidden behind the O club until darkness had fallen. He had even forsaken the pleasure of slitting Susan Turnbull's throat so as not to raise any alarm.

But as soon as he had arrived at the stash, he had been surrounded by dozens of special squad members, as though they had been waiting for him, which, it turned out, they had. Unbeknown to him a massive manhunt had been launched after Shane and the other Simon had been discovered missing from the prison. Apparently, the police had staked out the various haunts of the infamous pair and Simon had walked straight into their net.

Naturally, he had protested, saying that he was Bridge, but when he had mentioned Susan as his alibi, he had been informed that she, too, had been arrested. CC cameras showed her blatantly leaving the prison, withdrawing money, and even buying clothes for him. She had also dismissed her driver so they would be alone together.

As he sat there, about to spend the rest of his days at Her Majesty's pleasure, Simon recalled what had happened to him the day prior at the prison. He had sat there in the library waiting for Shane to arrive and bop him on his head. But after thirty minutes or so he realised that Shane wasn't coming and had furtively edged his way to the infirmary, poking his head around the corner to see Simon Mark One sitting there, smiling at him.

He remembered the moment, how he had felt. *The tricky bastard.* He had outwitted himself. It was him, Simon Mark Two, that was supposed to be the one sitting there, ready to be taken with Shane on their journey back to 1898. With his prior knowledge, he would have fucked up H G's plans by not taking her spiked drink, cutting her throat, and taking control of the DEMAT. *Fuck, what terror I would have created with that.* But as it was, he had had no alternative but to assume the role of Bridge and make the best of his freedom, using Shane's stash to finance his murderous adventures.

But despite all that went wrong, he harboured no resentment toward his counterpart, even though the stupid bastard had completely fucked everything up. He would have done the same thing, which of course he had, seeing that he was him after all.

The irony was that H G had been proven correct. Since it was now the ignorant Simon, Simon Mark One, who was accompanying Shane, he would do exactly as he, Simon Mark Two, had previously done. Follow the same predictive paths that would eventually lead to the unfortunate scenario he presently found himself in.

And because he was being returned to the prison *after* this situation had played out, he had no way of altering its path. Simon Mark One would have already left with H G and Shane, which meant that *he* would be the only version of himself present when he arrived back. Simon Mark One returning as Mark Two *prior* to H G, Shane, and him leaving in the first place. They were locked into an eternal time loop. He was helpless.

It seemed H G was to have her way after all. All their paths predestined.

The End

YOU MAY ALSO ENJOY THE FOLLOWING FROM EXTASY BOOKS INC:

The Program
Stephen Mottram

Excerpt

The tall lady shook Jennifer's hand before returning it to her trench coat, remaining silent.

Fuck, she is petrified.

"You spoke of corruption within the legal system. What do you have for me?"

She spoke hesitantly, with a low, alto tone. "The diversion program, are you aware of it?"

"I am."

"It is being abused, used for exploitative purposes by those in power."

"Exploitative? In what way?"

"Sexually, pornographically."

"Pornographically? Have you any proof?"

Her informant remained on edge, looking around nervously. "I was a victim. I have a story to tell, but I face a large prison sentence if I am exposed. That is why I am being so secretive."

"I see. So what is your story?"

"I was driving along, well under the speed limit, when a police wagon, you know, one of those divvy vans, turns his flashing lights on behind me. I pulled over. I thought nothing of it until the policeman walked up to me and ordered me to step out of my vehicle. Then without warning, he handcuffed my wrists behind me."

"Handcuffed you? What was your response?"

"I asked him what was going on and he told me was acting under information."

"Information? What did he mean by that?"

"I had no idea. I was terrified. I have never been in trouble before, not even a speeding fine."

"Then what happened?"

"He checked my glove box and pulled out a quantity of pills, drugs, in a plastic bag and starts reading me my rights."

"When did all this happen?"

"Four months ago. It has taken me some time to find the courage to contact you."

"Why is that? What happened to you?"

"I ended up spending ninety days in a private residence, restrained day and night."

"Fuck me. Who did this to you, and what reason did they give?"

"It is a so-called education course, part of a diversion program approved by a magistrate."

"Why on earth would you agree to that?"

The tall lady became emotional, sobbing as she continued. "I had no choice. It was either that or ten years in prison for drug trafficking."

"Trafficking?"

"Yes. Apparently, there is a prescribed level for the amount of the drug seized. If it is over that level, it becomes a trafficking charge rather than a possession charge. They said they would alter the amount of the drug seized and make it the lesser charge if I agreed to the diversion program."

"But what about your attorney? What did he say?"

"I wasn't allowed to talk to him. If I did, they said they would immediately charge me with trafficking, making me ineligible for the diversion program."

Christ. What bastards. The poor girl had no hope.

"So it was either take the program or fight the greater charge?" said Jennifer.

"Exactly. After informing me of this, they left me alone in the interview room. Gave me time to reflect."

"Who are they?"

"The policeman and an inspector. The inspector was the one in charge of the interview. Then, while I am sitting there, my hands still cuffed, a lawyer comes into the room, an expert on diversion programs. He was amazing, very friendly, calmed me down and advised me on my options. He recommended I take the diversion program."

"But did you tell him you were being framed?"

"I did, and he seemed astonished. But he said regardless, I should take the program. It is government approved so I would not be in any danger. The only condition was that I had to confess my guilt to the possession charge. So I agreed. I was so frightened." She started to sob again.

Jennifer reassured her. "That's okay. Try to relax. This is astonishing what you are telling me. So what happened with your employment, your friends, family?"

"You take leave without pay, but you are compensated by the program."

"They pay you?"

"Yes, plus they organise your financials for you. You know, paying bills, things like that while you are locked up. And you tell your family and friends that you have won a paid vacation. They are all so happy for you. You are told to pack your bags, and then a limo picks you up and delivers you to the residence."

"And where was it?"

"I don't know. The driver pulls over after a short while, cuffs and blindfolds and gags you with one of those ball gags. It was so surreal, having my mouth invaded like that, so fucking scary."

This is un-fucking-believable.

"So what are their names? Do you have any documentation?"

"Nothing at all, I have no proof."

"Surely you could prove you didn't take a vacation, that it was all bullshit."

"How? I don't even know where I was kept."

"You're right, of course. So how can I help you?"

"During my confinement, I overheard my warder on the phone. They all will be at a media event celebrating the success of the diversion program. That event is being held this week, which is why I have contacted you."

"I could go to that," said Jennifer, "and if you came with me, you could point them out to me."

The look of fear that came over her companion shocked Jennifer.

"I could never go near them again. After ninety days of restrained solitary confinement, my nerves are shot," she said, visibly shaken at the thought of meeting her captors again. "Plus they have that ten-year jail sentence hanging over my head. Apparently, there is no statute of limitations on such a charge. I must be very careful. I am already taking a huge risk talking to you."

"But I thought it was reduced to the lesser charge?"

"It was, but only if I keep my mouth shut. They make sure you know that when you are released. If they knew I was talking to you, I would be re-charged with trafficking."

Fucking bastards.

"That's okay," said Jennifer, "I don't need you. Can you give me a description of anyone, the policeman, the lawyer, the inspector?"

"The policeman, I will never forget him. He is pure evil.

He has short, white hair, like it's been bleached or some-thing. And his eyes, a piercing green, with prominent cheek-bones. I still have nightmares about him."

"He may not be at the function. He is only a constable. What about the inspector. What did he look like?"

"He's a short, stocky guy with a double chin."

"And the lawyer?"

"Oh, he's a charmer. Actually, I rather liked him. He's the one who calmed me down, made it all seem reasonable. He is very good looking, sharp. Well-cut suit with auburn hair and a charming smile."

Jennifer could see she was still charmed by this guy. So all I have to look for is a peroxide evil bastard, a stocky inspec-tor, and a red-headed charmer. Shouldn't be too difficult.

The tall lady spoke again. "The warder, she told me some-thing else."

"Yes?"

"She says I was selected because of my neat, ordered ap-pearance."

Fuck. Well, I will fit that bill perfectly. Already a plan was formulating in her brain.

"This warder, can you describe her?"

"Oh God yes, she's also unforgettable. A giant woman, six feet plus, of African descent. She is stunning and has very short, curly hair. She was very authoritative, but she was charming as well, almost sinister, if you could imagine." Jennifer's informant looked at her watch. "I have to go. I hope you find the bastards and expose them. You're good at that. That's why I contacted you."

She left abruptly, taking a stairwell doorway.

Jennifer climbed into her car, sitting there as she contem-plated what she had just heard.

What a story! This will make headlines around the coun-try, around the world even. I must get to that media event, track down these bastards.

She drove toward her home, thinking how best to approach this latest challenge. Somehow I have to become a victim. Present myself to them. And if she is to be believed, it has to be as neatly and as ordered as possible.

That, of course, was not a problem. It was as though her next assignment had been tailored for her.

What luck.

But Jennifer knew that the harder you worked, the luckier you got. And no one worked harder at their craft than her. To the extent she was prepared to immerse herself completely in her latest project, become their latest quarry.

But it will be me that is the stalker, and they my prey.

ABOUT THE AUTHOR

Stephen Mottram is a retired grandfather of three who lives in Melbourne Australia. After retiring Stephen re-educated himself, studying various subjects at a tertiary level, including philosophy, astronomy, fine drawing, and history. However, he draws most of his knowledge from his own very interesting life, a life where he explored his own humanity to the fullest, garnering many wonderful experiences and meeting some amazing people along the way. Stephen uses these life experiences in his writing, injecting a whimsical and informative style to all of his books. Gifting his readers with an individual and interesting perspective on humanity where he exposes both its wonderful frailties and its astonishing strengths.